W9-CUB-199

CONTEMPORARY AMERICAN FICTION

FEVER

Described by *The New York Times* as "one of America's premier writers of fiction," John Edgar Wideman published his first novel, *A Glance Away*, in 1967 at the age of twenty-six. His fifth novel, *Send for You Yesterday*, brought him the PEN/ Faulkner Award in 1983. His most recent novels are the widely acclaimed *Philadelphia Fire* (1990) and *Reuben* (1987). He is also the author of a memoir, *Brothers and Keepers*, which was nominated for the National Book Critics Circle Award in 1984. His other works of fiction are *Hurry Home* (1969), *The Lynchers* (1973), *Damballah* (1981), and *Hiding Place* (1981). He lives in Amherst and teaches at the University of Massachusetts.

FEVER

TWELVE STORIES

John
Edgar
Wideman

PENGUIN BOOKS

PENGUIN BOOKS
Published by the Penguin Group
Viking Penguin, a division of Penguin Books USA Inc.,
375 Hudson Street, New York, New York 10014, U.S.A.
Penguin Books Ltd, 27 Wrights Lane, London W8 5TZ, England
Penguin Books Australia Ltd, Ringwood, Victoria, Australia
Penguin Books Canada Ltd, 2801 John Street,
Markham, Ontario, Canada L3R 1B4
Penguin Books (N.Z.) Ltd, 182–190 Wairau Road, Auckland 10, New Zealand

Penguin Books Ltd, Registered Offices:
Harmondsworth, Middlesex, England

First published in the United States of America
by Henry Holt and Company, Inc., 1989
Reprinted by arrangement with Henry Holt and Company, Inc.
Published in Penguin Books 1990

1   3   5   7   9   10   8   6   4   2

"Doc's Story" first appeared in *Esquire*, vol. 106, no. 2 (August
1986); "Surfiction" first appeared in *The Southern Review*, vol.
21, no. 3 (Summer 1985); "When It's Time to Go" first appeared in *Callaloo*, vol. 4, nos. 1–3 (February–October 1981);
"Presents" first appeared in *River Styx*, no. 26; and "The Tambourine Lady" first appeared in *Iowa Review*, vol. 14, no. 1 (1984).

LIBRARY OF CONGRESS CATALOGING IN PUBLICATION DATA
Wideman, John Edgar.
Fever: twelve stories/John Edgar Wideman.
p.   cm. — (Contemporary American fiction)
Contents: Doc's story — The Statue of Liberty — Valaida —
Hostages — Surfiction — Rock River — When it's time to go —
Concert — Presents — The tambourine lady — Little brother —
Fever.
ISBN 0 14 01.4347 5
I. Title.   II. Series.
PS3573.I26F4   1990
813'.54—dc20   90–7015

Printed in the United States of America

To my aunts,
Geral, Martha, and Catherine
whose spirit is always in the work.

And to Andrew Wylie,
whose friendship and support
have been invaluable.

CONTENTS

FEVER

DOC'S STORY

He thinks of her small, white hands, blue veined, gaunt, awkwardly knuckled. He'd teased her about the smallness of her hands, hers lost in the shadow of his when they pressed them together palm to palm to measure. The heavy drops of color on her nails barely reached the middle joints of his fingers. He'd teased her about her dwarf's hands but he'd also said to her one night when the wind was rattling the windows of the apartment on Cedar and they lay listening and shivering though it was summer on the brass bed she'd found in a junk store on Haverford Avenue, near the Woolworth's five-and-dime they'd picketed for two years, that God made little things closer to perfect than he ever made big things. Small, compact women like her could be perfectly formed, proportioned, and he'd smiled out loud running his hand up and down the just-right fine lines of her body, celebrating how good she felt to him.

She'd left him in May, when the shadows and green of

the park had started to deepen. Hanging out, becoming a regular at the basketball court across the street in Regent Park was how he'd coped. No questions asked. Just the circle of stories. If you didn't want to miss anything good you came early and stayed late. He learned to wait, be patient. Long hours waiting were not time lost but time doing nothing because there was nothing better to do. Basking in sunshine on a stone bench, too beat to play any longer, nowhere to go but an empty apartment, he'd watch the afternoon traffic in Regent Park, dog strollers, baby carriages, winos, kids, gays, students with blankets they'd spread out on the grassy banks of the hollow and books they'd pretend to read, the black men from the neighborhood who'd search the park for braless young mothers and white girls on blankets who didn't care or didn't know any better than to sit with their crotches exposed. When he'd sit for hours like that, cooking like that, he'd feel himself empty out, see himself seep away and hover in the air, a fine mist, a little, flattened-out gray cloud of something wavering in the heat, a presence as visible as the steam on the window as he stares for hours at winter.

He's waiting for summer. For the guys to begin gathering on the court again. They'll sit in the shade with their backs against the Cyclone fencing or lean on cars parked at the roller-coaster curb or lounge in the sun on low, stone benches catty-corner from the basketball court. Some older ones still drink wine, but most everybody cools out on reefer, when there's reefer passed along, while they bullshit and wait for winners. He collects the stories they tell. He needs a story now. The right one now to get him through this long winter because she's gone and won't leave him alone.

In summer fine grit hangs in the air. Five minutes on

the court and you're coughing. City dirt and park dust blowing off bald patches from which green is long gone, and deadly ash blowing over from New Jersey. You can taste it some days, bitter in your spit. Chunks pepper your skin, burn your eyes. Early fall while it's still warm enough to run outdoors the worst time of all. Leaves pile up against the fence, higher and higher, piles that explode and jitterbug across the court in the middle of a game, then sweep up again, slamming back where they blew from. After a while the leaves are ground into coarse, choking powder. You eat leaf trying to get in a little hoop before the weather turns, before those days when nobody's home from work yet but it's dark already and too cold to run again till spring. Fall's the only time sweet syrupy wine beats reefer. Ripple, Manischewitz, Taylor's Tawny Port coat your throat. He takes a hit when the jug comes round. He licks the sweetness from his lips, listens for his favorite stories one more time before everybody gives it up till next season.

His favorite stories made him giggle and laugh and hug the others, like they hugged him when a story got so good nobody's legs could hold them up. Some stories got under his skin in peculiar ways. Some he liked to hear because they made the one performing them do crazy stuff with his voice and body. He learned to be patient, learned his favorites would be repeated, get a turn just like he got a turn on the joints and wine bottles circulating the edges of the court.

Of all the stories, the one about Doc had bothered him most. Its orbit was unpredictable. Twice in one week, then only once more last summer. He'd only heard Doc's story three times, but that was enough to establish Doc behind and between the words of all the other stories. In a strange way Doc presided over the court. You didn't need to mention him.

He was just there. Regent Park stories began with Doc and ended with Doc and everything in between was preparation, proof the circle was unbroken.

They say Doc lived on Regent Square, one of the streets like Cedar, dead-ending at the park. On the hottest afternoons the guys from the court would head for Doc's stoop. Jars of ice water, the good feeling and good talk they'd share in the shade of Doc's little front yard was what drew them. Sometimes they'd spray Doc's hose on one another. Get drenched like when they were kids and the city used to turn on fire hydrants in the summer. Some of Doc's neighbors would give them dirty looks. Didn't like a whole bunch of loud, sweaty, half-naked niggers backed up in their nice street where Doc was the only colored on the block. They say Doc didn't care. He was just out there like everybody else having a good time.

Doc had played at the University. Same one where Doc taught for a while. They say Doc used to laugh when white people asked him if he was in the Athletic Department. No reason for niggers to be at the University if they weren't playing ball or coaching ball. At least that's what white people thought, and since they thought that way, that's the way it was. Never more than a sprinkle of black faces in the white sea of the University. Doc used to laugh till the joke got old. People freedom-marching and freedom-dying, Doc said, but some dumb stuff never changed.

He first heard Doc's story late one day, after the yellow streetlights had popped on. Pooner was finishing the one about gang warring in North Philly: Yeah. They sure nuff lynched this dude they caught on their turf. Hung him up on the goddamn poles behind the backboard. Little kids found the sucker in the morning with his tongue all black and shit down his legs, and the cops had to come cut him down. Worst part

is them little kids finding a dead body swinging up there.
Kids don't be needing to find nothing like that. But those
North Philly gangs don't play. They don't even let the dead
rest in peace. Run in a funeral parlor and fuck up the funeral.
Dumping over the casket and tearing up the flowers. Scaring
people and turning the joint out. It's some mean shit. But
them gangs don't play. They kill you they ain't finished yet.
Mess with your people, your house, your sorry-ass dead body
to get even. Pooner finished telling it and he looked round at
the fellows and people were shaking their heads and then
there was a chorus of You got that right, man. It's a bitch
out there, man. Them niggers crazy, boy, and Pooner holds
out his hand and somebody passes the joint. Pooner pinches
it in two fingers and takes a deep drag. Everybody knows he's
finished, it's somebody else's turn.

   One of the fellows says, I wonder what happened to old
Doc. I always be thinking about Doc, wondering where the
cat is, what he be doing now . . .

   Don't nobody know why Doc's eyes start to going bad.
It just happen. Doc never even wore glasses. Eyes good as
anybody's far as anybody knew till one day he come round
he got goggles on. Like Kareem. And people kinda joking,
you know. Doc got him some goggles. Watch out, youall. Doc
be skyhooking youall to death today. Funning, you know.
Cause Doc like to joke and play. Doc one the fellas like I said,
so when he come round in goggles he subject to some teasing
and one another thing like that cause nobody thought nothing
serious wrong. Doc's eyes just as good as yours or mine, far
as anybody knew.

   Doc been playing all his life. That's why you could stand
him on the foul line and point him at the hoop and more
times than not, Doc could sink it. See he be remembering.

His muscles know just what to do. You get his feet aimed right, line him up so he's on target, and Doc would swish one for you. Was a game kinda. Sometimes you get a sucker and Doc win you some money. Swish. Then the cat lost the dough start crying. He ain't blind. Can't no blind man shoot no pill. Is you really blind, brother? You niggers trying to steal my money, trying to play me for a fool. When a dude start crying the blues like that Doc wouldn't like it. He'd walk away. Wouldn't answer.

Leave the man lone. You lost fair and square. Doc made the basket so shut up and pay up, chump.

Doc practiced. Remember how you'd hear him out here at night when people sleeping. It's dark but what dark mean to Doc? Blacker than the rentman's heart but don't make no nevermind to Doc, he be steady shooting fouls. Always be somebody out there to chase the ball and throw it back. But shit, man. When Doc into his rhythm, didn't need nobody chase the ball. Ball be swishing with that good backspin, that good arch bring it back blip, blip, blip, three bounces and it's coming right back to Doc's hands like he got a string on the pill. Spooky if you didn't know Doc or know about foul shooting and understand when you got your shit together don't matter if you blindfolded. You put the motherfucker up and you know it's spozed to come running back just like a dog with a stick in his mouth.

Doc always be hanging at the court. Blind as wood but you couldn't fool Doc. Eyes in his ears. Know you by your walk. He could tell if you wearing new sneaks, tell you if your old ones is laced or not. Know you by your breath. The holes you make in the air when you jump. Doc was hip to who fucking who and who was getting fucked. Who could play ball and who was jiving. Doc use to be out here every weekend,

steady rapping with the fellows and doing his foul-shot thing
between games. Every once in a while somebody tease him,
Hey, Doc. You want to run winners next go? Doc laugh and
say, No, Dupree ... I'm tired today, Dupree. Besides which
you ain't been on a winning team in a week have you, Du?
And everybody laugh. You know, just funning cause Doc one
the fellas.

But one Sunday the shit got stone serious. Sunday I'm
telling youall about, the action was real nice. If you wasn't
ready, get back cause the brothers was cooking. Sixteen points,
rise and fly. Next. Who got next? ... Come on out here and
take your ass kicking. One them good days when it's hot and
everybody's juices is high and you feel you could play till next
week. One them kind of days and a run's just over. Doc gets
up and he goes with Billy Moon to the foul line. Fellas hanging under the basket for the rebound. Ain't hardly gon be a
rebound Doc get hisself lined up right. But see, when the ball
drop through the net you want to be the one grab it and
throw it back to Billy. You want to be out there part of Doc
shooting fouls just like you want to run when the running's
good.

Doc bounce the ball, one, two, three times like he does.
Then he raise it. Sift it in his fingers. You know he's a ball-
player, a shooter already way the ball spin in them long fingers way he raises it and cocks his wrist. You know Doc can't
see a damn thing through his sunglasses but swear to God
you'd think he was looking at the hoop way he study and
measure. Then he shoots and ain't a sound in whole Johnson.
Seems like everybody's heart stops. Everybody's breath behind that ball pushing it and steadying it so it drops through
clean as new money.

But that Sunday something went wrong. Couldna been

wind cause wasn't no wind. I was there. I know. Maybe Doc had playing on his mind. Couldn't help have playing on his mind cause it was one those days wasn't nothing better to do in the world than play. Whatever it was, soon as the ball left his hands, you could see Doc was missing, missing real bad. Way short and way off to the left. Might hit the backboard if everybody blew on it real hard.

A young boy, one them skinny, jumping-jack young boys got pogo sticks for legs, one them kids go up and don't come back down till they ready, he was standing on the left side the lane and leap up all the sudden catch the pill out the air and jams it through. Blam. A monster dunk and everybody break out in Goddamn. Do it, Sky, and Did you see that nigger get up? People slapping five and all that mess. Then Sky, the young boy they call Sky, grinning like a Chessy cat and strutting out with the ball squeezed in one hand to give it to Doc. In his glory. Grinning and strutting.

Gave you a little help, Doc.

Didn't ask for no help, Sky. Why'd you fuck with my shot, Sky?

Well, up jumped the Devil. The joint gets real quiet again real quick. Doc ain't cracked smile the first. He ain't playing.

Sorry, Doc. Didn't mean no harm, Doc.

You must think I'm some kind of chump fucking with my shot that way.

People start to feeling bad. Doc is steady getting on Sky's case. Sky just a young, light-in-the-ass kid. Jump to the moon but he's just a silly kid. Don't mean no harm. He just out there like everybody else trying to do his thing. No harm in Sky but Doc ain't playing and nobody else says shit. It's quiet like when Doc's shooting. Quiet as death and Sky don't

know what to do. Can't wipe that lame look off his face and
can't back off and can't hand the pill to Doc neither. He just
stands there with his arm stretched out and his rusty fingers
wrapped round the ball. Can't hold it much longer, can't let
it go.

Seems like I coulda strolled over to Doc's stoop for a
drinka water and strolled back and those two still be standing
there. Doc and Sky. Billy Moon off to one side so it's just Doc
and Sky.

Everybody holding they breath. Everybody want it over
with and finally Doc says, Forget it, Sky. Just don't play with
my shots anymore. And then Doc say, Who has next winners?

If Doc was joking nobody took it for no joke. His voice
still hard. Doc ain't kidding around.

Who's next? I want to run.

Now Doc knows who's next. Leroy got next winners and
Doc knows Leroy always saves a spot so he can pick up a big
man from the losers. Leroy tell you to your face, I got my
five, man, but everybody know Leroy saving a place so he can
build him a winner and stay on the court. Leroy's a cold dude
that way, been that way since he first started coming round
and ain't never gon change and Doc knows that, everybody
knows that but even Leroy ain't cold enough to say no to Doc.

I got it, Doc.

You got your five yet?

You know you got a spot with me, Doc. Always did.

Then I'ma run.

Say to myself, Shit . . . Good God Almighty. Great Googa-
Mooga. What is happening here? Doc can't see shit. Doc
blind as this bench I'm sitting on. What Doc gon do out
there?

Well, it ain't my game. If it was, I'd a lied and said I

had five. Or maybe not. Don't know what I'da done, to tell
the truth. But Leroy didn't have no choice. Doc caught him
good. Course Doc knew all that before he asked.

Did Doc play? What kinda question is that? What you
think I been talking about all this time, man? Course he
played. Why the fuck he be asking for winners less he was
gon play? Helluva run as I remember. Overtime and shit.
Don't remember who won. Somebody did, sure nuff. Leroy
had him a strong unit. You know how he is. And Doc? Doc
ain't been out on the court for a while but Doc is Doc, you
know. Held his own ...

If he had tried to tell her about Doc, would it have made
a difference? Would the idea of a blind man playing basketball get her attention or would she have listened the way she
listened when he told her stories he'd read about slavery days
when Africans could fly, change themselves to cats and hum-
mingbirds, when black hoodoo priests and conjure queens were
feared by powerful whites even though ordinary black lives
weren't worth a penny. To her it was folklore, superstition.
Interesting because it revealed the psychology, the pathology
of the oppressed. She listened intently, not because she
thought she'd hear truth. For her, belief in magic was like
belief in God. Nice work if you could get it. Her skepticism,
her hardheaded practicality, like the smallness of her hands,
appealed to him. Opposites attracting. But more and more as
the years went by, he'd wanted her with him, wanted them to
be together ...

They were walking in Regent Park. It was clear to both
of them that things weren't going to work out. He'd never
seen her so beautiful, perfect.

There should have been stars. Stars at least, and perhaps
a sickle moon. Instead the edge of the world was on fire. They

were walking in Regent Park and dusk had turned the tree trunks black. Beyond them in the distance, below the fading blue of sky, the colors of sunset were pinched into a narrow, radiant band. Perhaps he had listened too long. Perhaps he had listened too intently for his own voice to fill the emptiness. When he turned back to her, his eyes were glazed, stinging. Grit, chemicals, whatever it was coloring, poisoning the sky, blurred his vision. Before he could blink her into focus, before he could speak, she was gone.

If he'd known Doc's story he would have said: *There's still a chance. There's always a chance. I mean this guy, Doc. Christ. He was stone blind. But he got out on the court and played. Over there. Right over there. On that very court across the hollow from us. It happened. I've talked to people about it many times. If Doc could do that, then anything's possible. We're possible . . .*

If a blind man could play basketball, surely we . . . If he had known Doc's story, would it have saved them? He hears himself saying the words. The ball arches from Doc's fingertips, the miracle of it sinking. Would she have believed any of it?

THE STATUE OF LIBERTY

One of the pleasures of jogging in the country is seeing those houses your route takes you past each day and wondering who lives in them. Some sit a good distance from the road, small, secluded by trees, tucked in a fold of land where they've been sheltered thousands of years from the worst things that happen to people. A little old couple lives in this kind. They've raised many children and lost some to the city but the family name's on mailboxes scattered up and down the road, kids and grandkids in houses like their folks', farmers like them, like more generations than you'd care to count back to England and cottages that probably resemble these, Capes, with roofs pulled down almost to the ground the way the old man stuffs on a wool cap bitter February days to haul in firewood from the shed. There are majestic hilltop-sitters with immaculate outbuildings and leaded glass and fine combed lawns sloping in every direction, landmarks you can measure your progress by as you reel in the countryside step by step jogging. I like best those ramshackle outfits—you can tell it's an old farm two young people from the city have taken over with their city dreams and city habits because it's not a real farm anymore, more somebody's idea of what living in the country should be at this day and time. A patched-together look, a corniness and coziness like pictures in a child's book, these city people have a little bit of everything growing on their few acres, and they keep goats, chickens, turkeys, ducks, geese, one cow—a pet zoo, really, and a German shepherd on a chain outside the trailer they've converted to a permanent dwelling. You know they smoke dope and let their kids run around naked as the livestock. They still blast loud city music on a stereo too big for the trailer and watch the stars through a kind of skylight contraption rigged in the tin roof and you envy them the time they first came out from the city, all those stars and nobody around but the two of them, starting out fresh in a different place and nothing better to do than moon up at the night sky and listen to the crickets and make each other feel nice in bed. Those kinds of houses must have been on your jogging route once. You look for them now beneath overloaded clotheslines, beyond rusted-out car stumps, in junk and mess and weeds, you can't tell what all's accumulated in the front yard from where you pass on the road.

A few houses close to the road. Fresh paint and shutters and shrubs, a clean-cut appearance and you think of suburbs, of neat house after house exactly alike, exactly like this one sitting solitary where it doesn't fit into the countryside. Retired people. Two frail old maids on canvas folding chairs in the attached garage with its wizard door rolled up and a puffy, ginger-colored cat crossing from one lady's stockinged feet to the other lady's stockinged feet like a conversation you can't hear from the road. Taking the air in their gazebo is what they're thinking in that suburban garage with its wide door open.

In the window of another one only a few yards from the road you can't tell if there's a person in the dark looking out because the panes haven't been washed in years. A house wearing sunglasses. You have a feeling someone very very old is still alive inside watching you, watching everything that passes, a face planted there in the dark so long, so patient and silent it scares you for no good reason. A gray, sprawled sooty clapboard swaybacked place a good wind could knock over but that wind hasn't blown through yet, not in all the time it's taken the man and woman who live here to shrivel up and crack and curl like the shingles on their steep roof that looks like a bad job of trying to paint a picture of the ocean, brushstrokes that don't become stormy ocean waves but stay brushstrokes, separate, unconnected, slapped on one after another in a hurry-up, hopeless manner that doesn't fool anyone.

A dim-shouldered, stout woman in a blue housedress with a lacy dirty white collar is who I imagine staring at me when I clomp-clomp-clomp by, straining on the slight grade that carries me beyond this house and barn people stopped painting fifty years ago, where people stopped living at least that long ago but they're too old now to die.

Once I thought of an eye large enough to fill the space inside those weather-beaten walls, under that slapdash roof. Just an eye. Self-sufficient. Enormous. White and veiny. Hidden in there with nothing else to do but watch.

Another way jogging pleasures me is how it lets me turn myself into another person in another place. The city, for instance. I'm small and pale running at night in a section of town I've been warned never to enter alone even in daylight.

I run burning with the secret of who I am, what I'm carrying, what I can do, secrets no one would guess just watching me jog past, a smallish, solitary white woman nearly naked on dangerous streets where she has no business being. She's crazy, they think. Or asking for it. But no one knows I can kill instantly, efficiently, with my fingers, toes and teeth. No one can see the tiny deadly weapons I've concealed on my person. In a wristband pouch. Under a Velcro flap in my running shorts. Nor would anyone believe the speed in my legs. No one can catch me unless I want to be caught.

When the huge black man springs from the shadows I let him grapple me to the ground. I tame him with my eyes. Instantly he understands. Nothing he could steal from me, throwing me down on the hard cement, hurting me, stripping me, mounting me with threats and his sweaty hand in my mouth so I won't scream, none of his violence, his rage, his hurry to split me and pound himself into me would bring the pleasure I'm ready to give of my own free will. I tell him with my eyes that I've been running to meet him. I jog along his dangerous streets because I'm prepared for him. He lets me undress him. I'm afraid for a moment his skin will be too black and I'll lose him in this dark alley. But my hands swim in the warmth of him. His smell, the damp sheen tells me he's been jogging too. It's peaceful where we are. We understand each other perfectly. Understand how we've been mistaken about each other for longer than we care to admit. Instead of destroying you, I whisper to him, I choose to win you with the gentleness in my eyes. Convert you. Release you. Then we can invent each other this quiet way, breath by breath, limb by limb, as if we have all the time in the world and our bodies are a route we learn jogging leisurely till the route's inside us, imagining us, our bodies carried along by it effortlessly.

We stand and trot off shoulder to shoulder. He has Doberman legs. They twirl as if on a spit.

For weeks now they've been going by each morning. Crooker hears them first. Yapping and thrashing, running the length of her chain till it yanks her back to reality. A loud, stupid dog. I think she believes she's going to escape each time she takes a dash at her chain. She barks and snarls at them and I'd like to rubber-band her big mouth shut.

Quiet, Crooker. Hush.

Leave her be, Orland grumps to me. Barking's her job. She gets fed to bark.

We both know Crooker's useless as a watchdog. She growls at her reflection in the French doors. She howls at birds a mile away. A bug can start her yelping. Now she's carrying on as if the Beast from Babylon's slouching down the road to eat us all for breakfast and it's nobody but the joggers she's seen just like I've seen them every morning for a week. Passing by, shading to the other edge of the road because they don't want to aggravate a strange, large country dog into getting so frantic it just might snap its chain.

Nothing but those joggers she's barking at. Shut up, Crooker.

How do you know those people ain't the kind to come back snooping around here at night? Pacify the dog and them or others like them be right up on top of us before we know it.

Orland, please. What in the world are you grumbling about? You're as bad as she is.

I pay her to bark. Let her bark.

She's Crooker because at birth her tail didn't come out right. An accident in the womb. Her tail snagged on something and it's been crook-ended since. Poor creature couldn't even walk through the door of life right. But she was lucky too. Molly must have been spooked by the queerness of that tail. Must have been the humped tail because Molly ate every other pup in that litter. Ate them before we caught on and rescued this crook-tailed one.

When they pass by the window Orland doesn't even glance up. He doesn't know what he's missing. Usually he's gone long before they jog past. I forget what kept him late the morning I'm recalling. It's not that he's a hard worker or busy or conscientious. For years now the point's been to rise early and be gone. Gone the important part. Once he's gone he can figure out some excuse for going, some excuse to keep himself away. I think he may have another place where he sleeps. Tucks himself in again after he leaves my bed and dreams half the day away like a baby. Orland misses them. Might as well be a squirrel or moth riling Crooker. If he knew the woman looked as good as she does in her silky running shorts, he'd sure pay attention. If he knew the man was a big black man his stare would follow mine out the window and pay even more attention.

They seem to be about my age more or less. Woman rather short but firm and strong with tight tanned legs from jogging. She packs a bit more weight in the thighs than I do, but I haven't gained an inch anywhere nor a pound since I was a teenager. My face betrays me, but I was blessed with a trim, athletic high school beauty queen's figure. Even after the first two children Orland swore at me once when he pulled off my nightie, Damned Jailbait.

The man's legs from ankle to the fist of muscle before the knee are straight and hard as pipes, bony as dog's legs then flare into wedges of black thigh, round black man's butt. First morning I was with the kids in the front yard he waved.

A big hello-how-are-you smiling-celebrity wave the way black men make you think they're movie stars or professional athletes with a big, wide wave, like you should know them if you don't and that momentary toothy spotlight they cast on you is something special from that big world where they're famous. He's waved every morning since. When I've let him see me. I know he looks for me. I wasn't wearing much more than the kids when he saw me in the yard. I know he wonders if I stroll around the house naked or sunbathe in the nude on a recliner behind the house in the fenced yard you can't see from the road. I've waited with my back close enough to the bedroom window so he'd see me if he was trying, a bare white back he could spot even though it's hard to see inside this gloomy house that hour in the morning. A little reward, if he's alert. I shushed Crooker and smiled back at him, up at him the first time, kneeling beside Billy, tying my Billyboy's shoe. We're complete smiling buddies now and the woman greets me too.

No doubt about it he liked what he saw. Three weeks now and they'd missed only two Sundays and an odd Thursday. Three times it had rained. I didn't count those days. Never do. Cooped up in the house with four children under nine you wouldn't waste your time or energy either, counting rainy, locked-in days like that because you need every ounce of patience, every speck of will, just to last to bedtime. Theirs. Which on rainy cooped-up days is followed immediately by yours because you're whipped, fatigued, bone and brain tired living in a child's world of days with no middle, end or beginning, just time like some Silly Putty you're stuck in the belly of. You can't shape it; it shapes you, but the shape is no real shape at all, it's the formlessness of no memory, no sleep that won't let you get a handle on anything, let you be anything but whatever it is twisted, pulled, worried. Three weeks minus three minus days that never count anyway minus one Thursday minus twice they perhaps went to church and that equals what? Equals the days required for us to become acquainted. To get past curiosity into *Hi there*. To follow up his presidential candidate's grin and high-five salute with my cheeriness, my punch-clock punctuality, springing tick-tock from my gingerbread house so I'm in sight, available, when they jog by. Most of the time, apparently. Always, if he takes the trouble to seek me out. As if the two of them, the tall black man and his shortish, tanned white lady companion, were yoked together, pulling the sun around the world and the two of them had been circling the globe forever, in step, in time with each other, round and round like the tiger soup in a Little Black Sambo book I read to my children, achieving a rhythm, a high-stepping pace unbroken and sufficient unto itself but I managed to blend in, to jog beside them invisible till I learned their pace and rhythm, flowing, unobtrusive, even when they both discovered me there, braced with them, running with them, undeniably part of whatever they think they are doing every morning when they pass my house and wave.

He liked what he saw because when they finally did stop and come in for the cool drinks I'd proposed first as a kind of joke, then a standing offer, seriously, no trouble, whenever, if ever, they choose to stop, then on a tray, two actual frosty tumblers of ice water they couldn't refuse without hurting my feelings, he took his and brushed my fingertips in a gesture that wasn't accidental, he wasn't a clumsy man, he took a glass and half my finger with it because he'd truly liked what he saw and admired it more close up.

Sweat sheen gleamed on him like a fresh coat of paint.

He was pungent as tar. I could smell her mixed in with him. They'd made love before they jogged. Hadn't bothered to bathe before starting off on their route. She didn't see me remove my halter. He did. I sat him where he'd have to force himself to look away in order not to see me slip the halter over my head. I couldn't help standing, my arms raised like a prisoner of war, letting him take his own good time observing the plump breasts that are the only part of my anatomy below my neck not belonging to a fourteen-year-old girl. She did not see what I'd done till I turned the corner, but she seemed not to notice or not to care. I didn't need to use the line I'd rehearsed in front of the mirror, the line that went with my stripper's curtsy, with my arm stretched like Miss Liberty over my head and my wrist daintily cocked, dangling in my fingers the wisp of halter: We're very casual around here.

Instead, as we sit sipping our ice waters I laugh and say, This weather's too hot for clothes. I tease my lips with the tip of my tongue. I roll the frosted glass on my breasts. This feels so nice. Let me do you. I push up her tank top. Roll the glass on her flat stomach.

You're both so wet. Why don't you get off those damp things and sit out back? Cool off awhile. It's perfectly private.

I'll fetch us more drinks. Not too early for something stronger than water, is it?

They exchange easily deciphered looks. For my benefit, speaking to me as much as to each other. Who is this woman? What the hell have we gotten ourselves into?

I guide her up from the rattan chair. It's printed ruts across the backs of her thighs. My fingers are on her elbow. I slide open the screen door and we step onto the unfinished mess of flagstone, mismatched tile and brick Orland calls a patio. The man lags behind us. He'll see me from the rear as I balance on one leg then the other, stepping out of my shorts.

I point her to one of the lawn chairs.

Make yourself comfortable. Orland and the kids are gone for the day. Just the three of us. No one else for miles. It's glorious. Pull off your clothes, stretch out and relax.

I turn quickly and catch him liking what he sees, all of me naked, but he's wary. A little shocked. All of this too good to be true. I don't allow him time to think overly long about it.

You're joining us, aren't you? No clothes allowed.

After I plop down I watch out of the corner of my eye how she wiggles and kicks out of her shorts, her bikini underwear. Her elasticized top comes off over her head. Arms raised in that gesture of surrender every woman performs shrugging off what's been hiding her body. She's my sister then. I remember myself in the mirror of her. Undressing just a few minutes before, submitting, taking charge.

Crooker howls from the pen where I've stuffed her every morning since the first week. She'd been quiet till his long foot in his fancy striped running shoe touched down on the patio. Her challenge scares him. He freezes, framed a moment in the French doors.

It's OK. She's locked in her pen. All she'd do if she were here is try to lick you to death. C'mon out.

I smile over at the woman. Aren't men silly most of the time? Under that silence, those hard stares, that playacting that's supposed to be a personality, aren't they just chicken-hearted little boys most of the time? She knows exactly what I'm thinking without me saying a word. Men. Her black man no different from the rest.

He slams the screen door three times before it catches in the glides that haven't been right since Orland set them. The man can't wait to see the two of us, sisters again because I've assumed the same stiff posture in my lawn chair as she has in hers, back upright, legs extended straight ahead, ankles crossed. We are as demure as two white ladies can be in broad daylight displayed naked for the eyes of a black man. Her breasts are girlish, thumb nippled. Her bush a fuzzy creature in her lap. I'm as I promised. He'll like what he'll see, can't wait to see, but he's pretending to be in no hurry, undoing his bulky shoes lace by lace instead of kicking them off his long feet. The three chairs are arranged in a Y, foot ends converging. I steered her where I wanted her and took my seat so he'll be in the middle, facing us both, her bare flesh or mine everywhere he turns. With all his heart, every hidden fiber he wants to occupy the spot I've allotted for him, but he believes if he seems in too much of a rush, shows undue haste, he'll embarrass himself, reveal himself for what he is, what he was when Crooker's bark stopped him short.

He manages a gangly nonchalance, settling down, shooting out his legs so the soles of three pairs of feet would kiss if we inched just a wee bit closer to the bull's-eye. His shins gleam like black marble. When he's jogging he flows. Up close I'm aware of joints, angles, hinges, the struts and wires of sinew assembling him, the patchwork of his dark skin, many colors, like hers, like mine, instead of the tar-baby sleekness that trots past my window. His palms, the pale underpads of his feet have no business being the blank, clownish color they are. She could wear that color on her hands and feet and he could wear hers and the switch would barely be noticeable.

We're in place now and she closes her eyes, leans back her head and sighs. It is quiet and nice here. So peaceful, she says. This is a wonderful idea, she says, and teaches herself how to recline, levers into prone position and lays back so we're no longer three wooden Indians.

My adjustment is more subtle. I drop one foot on either side of my chair so I'm straddling it, then scoot the chair with me on it a few inches to change the angle the sun strikes my face. An awkward way to move, a lazy, stuttering adjustment useful only because it saves me standing up. And it's less than modest. My knees are spread the width of the lawn chair as I ride it to a new position. If the man has liked what he's seen so far, and I know he has, every morsel, every crumb, then he must certainly be pleased by this view. I let him sink deeper. Raise my feet back to the vinyl strips of the leg rest, but keep my knees open, yawning, draw them towards my chest, hug them, snuggle them. Her tan is browner than mine. Caramel then cream where a bikini shape is saved on her skin. I show him the bottom of me is paler, but not much paler than my thighs, my knees I peer over, knees like two big scoops of coffee ice cream I taste with the tip of my tongue.

I'm daydreaming some of the things I'll let them do to me. Tie my limbs to the bed's four corners. Kneel me, spread the cheeks of my ass. I'll suck him while her fingers ply me. When it's the black man's turn to be bondaged and he's trussed up too tight to grin, Orland bursts through the bedroom door, chain saw cradled across his chest. No reason not to let everything happen. They are clean. In good health. My body's still limber and light as a girl's. They like what they see. She's pretending to nap but I know she can sense his eyes shining, the veins thickening in his rubbery penis as it stirs and arches between his thighs he presses together so it doesn't rear up and stab at me, single me out impolitely when there are two of us, two women he must take his time with and please. We play our exchange of smiles, him on the road, me with Billy and Sarah and Carl and Augie at the edge of our corn patch. I snare his eyes, lead them down slowly to my pearly bottom, observe myself there, finger myself, study what I'm showing him so when I raise my eyes and bring his up with me again, we'll both know beyond a doubt what I've been telling him every morning when he passes is true.

No secrets now. What do you see, you black bastard? My pubic hair is always cropped close and neat, a perfect triangle decorates the fork of the Y, a Y like the one I formed with our lawn chairs. I unclasp my knees, let them droop languorously apart, curl my toes on the tubing that frames my chair. She may be watching too. But it's now or never. We must move past certain kinds of resistance, habits that are nothing more than habits. Get past or be locked like stupid baying animals in a closet forever. My eyes challenge his. Yes those are the leaves of my vagina opening. Different colors inside than outside. Part of what's inside me unfolding, exposed, like the lips of your pouty mouth.

The petals of my vagina are two knuckles spreading of a fist stuck in your face. They are the texture of the softest things you've ever touched. Softer. Better. Fleece bedding them turns subtly damp. A musk rises, gently, magically, like the mist off the oval pond that must be included in your route if you jog very far beyond my window. But you may arrive too late or too early to have noticed. About a half mile from here the road climbs as steeply as it does in this rolling countryside. Ruins of a stone wall, an open field on the right, a ragged screen of pine trees borders the other side and if you peer through them, green of meadow is broken just at the foot of a hill by a black shape difficult to distinguish from dark tree trunks and their shadows, but search hard, it rests like a mirror into which a universe has collapsed. At dawn, at dusk the pond breathes. You can see when the light and air are right, something rare squeezed up from the earth's center, hanging over this pond. I believe a ghost with long, trailing hair is marooned there and if I ever get my courage up, I've promised myself I'll go jogging past at night and listen to her sing.

VALAIDA

Whither shall I go from thy spirit?
Or whither shall I flee from thy presence?

Bobby tell the man what he wants to hear. Bobby lights a
cigarette. Blows smoke and it rises and rises to where I sit on
my cloud overhearing everything. Singing to no one. Golden
trumpet from the Queen of Denmark across my knees. In my
solitude. Dead thirty years now and meeting people still.
Primping loose ends of my hair. Worried how I look. How I
sound. Silly. Because things don't change. Bobby with your
lashes a woman would kill for, all cheekbones, bushy brows
and bushy upper lip, ivory when you smile. As you pretend to
contemplate his jive questions behind your screen of smoke
and summon me by rolling your big, brown-eyed-handsome-
man eyeballs to the ceiling where smoke pauses not one instant, but scoots through and warms me where I am, tell him,
Bobby, about "fabled Valaida Snow who traveled in an orchid-
colored Mercedes-Benz, dressed in an orchid suit, her pet
monkey rigged out in an orchid jacket and cap, with the
chauffeur in orchid as well." If you need to, lie like a rug,

Bobby. But don't waste the truth, either. They can't take that away from me. Just be cool. As always. Recite those countries and cities we played. Continents we conquered. Roll those faraway places with strange-sounding names around in your sweet mouth. Tell him they loved me at home too, a down-home girl from Chattanooga, Tennessee, who turned out the Apollo, not a mumbling word from wino heaven till they were on their feet hollering and clapping for more with the rest of the audience. Reveries of days gone by, yes, yes, they haunt me, baby, I can taste it. Yesteryears, yesterhours. Bobby, do you also remember what you're not telling him? Blues lick in the middle of a blind flamenco singer's moan. Mother Africa stretching her crusty, dusky hands forth, calling back her far-flung children. Later that same night both of us bad on bad red wine wheeling round and round a dark gypsy cave. Olé. Olé.

Don't try too hard to get it right, he'll never understand. He's watching your cuff links twinkle. Wondering if they're real gold and the studs real diamonds. You called me Minnie Mouse. But you never saw me melted down to sixty-eight pounds soaking wet. They beat me, and fucked me in every hole I had. I was their whore. Their maid. A stool they stood on when they wanted to reach a little higher. But I never sang in their cage, Bobby. Not one note. Cost me a tooth once, but not a note. Tell him that one day I decided I'd had enough and walked away from their hell. Walked across Europe, the Atlantic Ocean, the whole U.S. of A. till I found a quiet spot put peace back in my soul, and then I began performing again. My tunes. In my solitude. And yes. There was a pitiful little stomped-down white boy in the camp I tried to keep the guards from killing, but if he lived or died I never knew. Then or now. Monkey and chauffeur and limo and champagne and cigars and outrageous dresses with rhinestones, fringe and peekaboo slits. That's the foolishness the reporter's after. Stuff him with your MC b.s., and if he's still curious when you're finished, if he seems a halfway decent sort in spite of himself, you might suggest listening to the trumpet solo in My Heart Belongs to Daddy, *hip him to* Hot Snow, *the next to last cut, my voice and Lady Day's figure and ground, ground and figure* Dear Lord above, send back my love.

He heard her in the bathroom, faucets on and off, on and off, spurting into the sink bowl, the tub. Quick burst of shower spray, rain sound spattering plastic curtain. Now in the quiet she'll be polishing. Every fixture will gleam. *Shine's what people see. See something shiny, don't look no further, most people don't.* If she's rushed she'll wipe and polish faucets, mirrors, metal collars around drains. Learned that trick when she first came to the city and worked with gangs of girls in big downtown hotels. *Told me, said, Don't be fussing around behind in there or dusting under them things, child. Give that mirror a lick. Rub them faucets. Twenty more rooms like this one here still to do before noon.* He lowers the newspaper just enough so he'll see her when she passes through the living room, so she won't see him looking unless she stops and stares, something she never does. She knows he watches. Let him know just how much was enough once upon a time when she first started coming to clean the apartment. Back when he was still leaving for work some mornings. Before they understood each other, when suspicions were mutual and thick as the dust first time she bolted through his doorway, into his rooms, out of breath and wary eyed like someone was chasing her and it might be him.

She'd burst in his door and he'd felt crowded. Retreated, let her stake out the space she required. She didn't bully him but demanded in the language of her brisk, efficient movements that he accustom himself to certain accommodations. They developed an etiquette that spelled out precisely how close, how distant the two of them could be once a week while she cleaned his apartment.

Odd that it took him years to realize how small she was. Shorter than him and no one in his family ever stood higher than five foot plus an inch or so of that thick, straight, black hair. America a land of giants and early on he'd learned to ignore height. You couldn't spend your days like a country lout gawking at the skyscraper heads of your new countrymen. No one had asked him so he'd never needed to describe his cleaning woman. Took no notice of her height. Her name was Clara Jackson and when she arrived he was overwhelmed by the busyness of her presence. How much she seemed to be doing all at once. Noises she'd manufacture with the cleaning paraphernalia, her humming and singing, the gum she popped, heavy thump of her heels even though she changed into tennis sneakers as soon as she crossed the threshold of his apartment, her troubled breathing, asthmatic wheezes and snorts of wrecked sinuses getting worse and worse over the years, her creaking knees, layers of dresses, dusters, slips whispering, the sighs and moans and wincing ejaculations, addresses to invisible presences she smuggled with her into his domain. *Yes, Lord. Save me, Jesus. Thank you, Father.* He backed away from the onslaught, the clamorous weight of it, avoided her systematically. Seldom were they both in the same room at the same time more than a few minutes because clearly none was large enough to contain them and the distance they needed.

She was bent over, replacing a scrubbed rack in the oven
when he'd discovered the creases in her skull. She wore a net
over her hair like serving girls in Horn and Hardart's. Under
the webbing were clumps of hair, defined by furrows exposing
her bare scalp. A ribbed yarmulke of hair pressed down on
top of her head. Hair he'd never imagined. Like balled yarn
in his grandmother's lap. Like a nursery rhyme. *Black sheep.
Black sheep, have you any wool?* So different from what grew
on his head, the heads of his brothers and sisters and mother
and father and cousins and everyone in the doomed village
where he was born, so different that he could not truly consider it hair, but some ersatz substitute used the evening of
creation when hair ran out. Easier to think of her as bald.
Bald and wearing a funny cap fashioned from the fur of some
swarthy beast. Springy wires of it jutted from the netting. One
dark strand left behind, shocking him when he discovered it
marooned in the tub's gleaming, white belly, curled like a
question mark at the end of the sentence he was always asking
himself. He'd pinched it up in a wad of toilet paper, flushed
it away.

Her bag of fleece had grayed and emptied over the years.
Less of it now. He'd been tempted countless times to touch
it. Poke his finger through the netting into one of the mounds.
He'd wondered if she freed it from the veil when she went to
bed. If it relaxed and spread against her pillow or if she slept
all night like a soldier in a helmet.

When he stood beside her or behind her he could spy
on the design of creases, observe how the darkness was cultivated into symmetrical plots and that meant he was taller than
Clara Jackson, that he was looking down at her. But those
facts did not calm the storm of motion and noise, did not
undermine her power any more than the accident of growth,

the half inch he'd attained over his next tallest brother, the inch eclipsing the height of his father, would have diminished his father's authority over the family, if there had been a family, the summer after he'd shot up past everyone, at thirteen the tallest, the height he remained today.

Mrs. Clara. Did you know a colored woman once saved my life?

Why is she staring at him as if he's said, Did you know I slept with a colored woman once? He didn't say that. Her silence fusses at him as if he did, as if he'd blurted out something unseemly, ungentlemanly, some insult forcing her to tighten her jaw and push her tongue into her cheek, and taste the bitterness of the hard lump inside her mouth. Why is she ready to cry, or call him a liar, throw something at him or demand an apology or look right through him, past him, the way his mother stared at him on endless October afternoons, gray slants of rain falling so everybody's trapped indoors and she's cleaning, cooking, tending a skeletal fire in the hearth and he's misbehaving, teasing his little sister till he gets his mother's attention and then he shrivels in the weariness of those sad eyes catching him in the act, piercing him, ignoring him, the hurt, iron and distance in them accusing him. Telling him for this moment, and perhaps forever, for this cruel, selfish trespass, you do not exist.

No, Mistah Cohen. That's one thing I definitely did not know.

His fingers fumble with a button, unfastening the cuff of his white shirt. He's rolling up one sleeve. Preparing himself for the work of storytelling. She has laundered the shirt how many times. It's held together by cleanliness and starch. A shirt that ought to be thrown away but she scrubs and sprays and irons it; he knows the routine, the noises. She saves it how many times, patching, mending, snipping errant threads, the frayed edges of cuff and collar hardened again so he is decent, safe within them, the blazing white breast he puffs out like a penguin when it's spring and he descends from the twelfth floor and conquers the park again, shoes shined, the remnants of that glorious head of hair slicked back, freshly shaved cheeks raw as a baby's in the brisk sunshine of those first days welcoming life back and yes he's out there in it again, his splay-foot penguin walk and gentleman's attire, shirt like a pledge, a promise, a declaration framing muted stripes of his dark tie. Numbers stamped inside the collar. Mark of the dry cleaners from a decade ago, before Clara Jackson began coming to clean. Traces still visible inside the neck of some of his shirts she's maintained impossibly long past their prime, a row of faded numerals like those he's pushing up his sleeve to show her on his skin.

The humped hairs on the back of his forearm are pressed down like grass in the woods where a hunted animal has slept. Gray hairs the color of his flesh, except inside his forearm, just above his wrist, the skin is whiter, blue veined. All of it, what's gray, what's pale, what's mottled with dark spots is meat that turns to lard and stinks a sweet sick stink to high heaven if you cook it.

Would you wish to stop now? Sit down a few minutes, please. I will make a coffee for you and my tea. I tell you a story. It is Christmas soon, no?

She is stopped in her tracks. A tiny woman, no doubt about it. Lumpy now. Perhaps she steals and hides things under her dress. Lumpy, not fat. Her shoulders round and padded. Like the derelict women who live in the streets and wear their whole wardrobes winter spring summer fall. She has put on flesh for protection. To soften blows. To ease

around corners. Something cushioned to lean against. Something to muffle the sound of bones breaking when she falls.
A pillow for all the heads gone and gone to dust who still find
ways at night to come to her and seek a resting place. He
could find uses for it. Extra flesh on her bones was not excess,
was a gift. The female abundance, her thickness, her bulk
reassuring as his hams shrink, his fingers become claws, the
chicken neck frets away inside those razor-edged collars she
scrubs and irons.

Oh you scarecrow. Death's-head stuck on a stick. Another
stick lashed crossways for arms. First time you see yourself
dead you giggle. You are a survivor, a lucky one. You grin,
stick out your tongue at the image in the shard of smoky glass
because the others must be laughing, can't help themselves,
the ring of them behind your back, peeking over your scrawny
shoulders, watching as you discover in the mirror what they've
been seeing since they stormed the gates and kicked open the
sealed barracks door and rescued you from the piles of live
kindling that were to be your funeral pyre. Your fellow men.
Allies. Victors. Survivors. Who stare at you when they think
you're not looking, whose eyes are full of shame, as if they've
been on duty here, in this pit, this stewpot cooking the meat
from your bones. They cannot help themselves. You laugh to
help them forget what they see. What you see. When they
herded your keepers past you, their grand uniforms shorn of
buttons, braid, ribbons, medals, the twin bolts of frozen light-
ning, golden skulls, eagles' wings, their jackboots gone, feet
bare or in peasant clogs, heads bowed and hatless, iron faces
unshaven, the butchers still outweighed you a hundred pounds
a man. You could not conjure up the spit to mark them. You
dropped your eyes in embarrassment, pretended to nod off
because your body was too weak to manufacture a string of

spittle, and if you could have, you'd have saved it, hoarded and tasted it a hundred times before you swallowed the precious bile.

A parade of shambling, ox-eyed animals. They are marched past you, marched past open trenches that are sewers brimming with naked, rotting flesh, past barbed-wire compounds where the living sift slow and insubstantial as fog among the heaps of dead. No one believes any of it. Ovens and gas chambers. Gallows and whipping posts. Shoes, shoes, shoes, a mountain of shoes in a warehouse. Shit. Teeth. Bones. Sacks of hair. The undead who huddle into themselves like bats and settle down on a patch of filthy earth mourning their own passing. No one believes the enemy. He is not these harmless farmers filing past in pillaged uniforms to do the work of cleaning up this mess someone's made. No one has ever seen a ghost trying to double itself in a mirror so they laugh behind its back, as if, as if the laughter is a game and the dead one could muster up the energy to join in and be made whole again. I giggle. I say, Who in God's name would steal a boy's face and leave this thing?

Nearly a half century of rich meals with seldom one missed but you cannot fill the emptiness, cannot quiet the clamor of those lost souls starving, the child you were, weeping from hunger, those selves, those stomachs you watched swelling, bloating, unburied for days and you dreamed of opening them, of taking a spoon to whatever was growing inside because you were so empty inside and nothing could be worse than that gnawing emptiness. Why should the dead be ashamed to eat the dead? Who are their brothers, sisters, themselves? You hear the boy talking to himself, hallucinating milk, bread, honey. Sick when the spoiled meat is finally carted away.

Mistah Cohen, I'm feeling kinda poorly today. If you don
mind I'ma work straight through and gwan home early. Got
all my Christmas still to do and I'm tired.

She wags her head. Mumbles more he can't decipher. As
if he'd offered many times before, as if there is nothing strange
or special this morning at 10:47, him standing at the china
cupboard prepared to open it and bring down sugar bowl, a
silver cream pitcher, cups and saucers for the two of them,
ready to fetch instant coffee, a tea bag, boil water and sit
down across the table from her. As if it happens each day she
comes, as if this once is not the first time, the only time he's
invited this woman to sit with him and she can wag her old
head, stare at him moon eyed as an owl and refuse what's
never been offered before.

The tattoo is faint. From where she's standing, fussing
with the vacuum cleaner, she won't see a thing. Her eyes, in
spite of thick spectacles, watery and weak as his. They have
grown old together, avoiding each other in these musty rooms
where soon, soon, no way round it, he will wake up dead one
morning and no one will know till she knocks Thursday, and
knocks again, then rings, pounds, hollers, but no one answers
and she thumps away to rouse the super with his burly ring
of keys.

He requires less sleep as he ages. Time weighs more on
him as time slips away, less and less time as each second
passes but also more of it, the past accumulating in vast drifts
like snow in the darkness outside his window. In the wolf
hours before dawn this strange city sleeps as uneasily as he
does, turning, twisting, groaning. He finds himself listening
intently for a sign that the night knows he's listening, but
what he hears is his absence. The night busy with itself, de-
nying him. And if he is not out there, if he can hear plainly

his absence in the night pulse of the city, where is he now, where was he before his eyes opened, where will he be when the flutter of breath and heart stop?

They killed everyone in the camps. The whole world was dying there. Not only Jews. People forget. All kinds locked in the camps. Yes. Even Germans who were not Jews. Even a black woman. Not gypsy. Not African. American like you, Mrs. Clara.

They said she was a dancer and could play any instrument. Said she could line up shoes from many countries and hop from one pair to the next, performing the dances of the world. They said the Queen of Denmark had honored her with a gold trumpet. But she was there, in hell with the rest of us.

A woman like you. Many years ago. A lifetime ago. Young then as you would have been. And beautiful. As I believe you must have been, Mrs. Clara. Yes. Before America entered the war. Already camps had begun devouring people. All kinds of people. Yet she was rare. Only woman like her I ever saw until I came here, to this country, this city. And she saved my life.

Poor thing.

I was just a boy. Thirteen years old. The guards were beating me. I did not know why. Why? They didn't need a why. They just beat. And sometimes the beating ended in death because there was no reason to stop, just as there was no reason to begin. A boy. But I'd seen it many times. In the camp long enough to forget why I was alive, why anyone would want to live for long. They were hurting me, beating the life out of me but I was not surprised, expected no explanation. I remember curling up as I had seen a dog once cowering from the blows of a rolled newspaper. In the old country lifetimes ago. A boy in my village staring at a dog curled and rolling on its back in the dust outside the baker's shop and our baker in his white apron and tall white hat striking this mutt again and again. I didn't know what mischief the dog had done. I didn't understand why the fat man with flour on his apron was whipping it unmercifully. I simply saw it and hated the man, felt sorry for the animal, but already the child in me understood it could be no other way so I rolled and curled myself against the blows as I'd remembered that spotted dog in the dusty village street because that's the way it had to be.

Then a woman's voice in a language I did not comprehend reached me. A woman angry, screeching. I heard her before I saw her. She must have been screaming at them to stop. She must have decided it was better to risk dying than watch the guards pound a boy to death. First I heard her voice, then she rushed in, fell on me, wrapped herself around me. The guards shouted at her. One tried to snatch her away. She wouldn't let go of me and they began to beat her too. I heard the thud of clubs on her back, felt her shudder each time a blow was struck.

She fought to her feet, dragging me with her. Shielding me as we stumbled and slammed into a wall.

My head was buried in her smock. In the smell of her, the smell of dust, of blood. I was surprised how tiny she was, barely my size, but strong, very strong. Her fingers dug into my shoulders, squeezing, gripping hard enough to hurt me if I hadn't been past the point of feeling pain. Her hands were strong, her legs alive and warm, churning, churning as she pressed me against herself, into her. Somehow she'd pulled me up and back to the barracks wall, propping herself, supporting me, sheltering me. Then she screamed at them in this language I use now but did not know one word of then, cursing them, I'm sure, in her mother tongue, a stream of spit

and sputtering sounds as if she could build a wall of words
they could not cross.

The kapos hesitated, astounded by what she'd dared.
Was this black one a madwoman, a witch? Then they tore me
from her grasp, pushed me down and I crumpled there in the
stinking mud of the compound. One more kick, a numbing,
blinding smash that took my breath away. Blood flooded my
eyes. I lost consciousness. Last I saw of her she was still fighting, slim, beautiful legs kicking at them as they dragged and
punched her across the yard.

You say she was colored?

Yes. Yes. A dark angel who fell from the sky and
saved me.

Always thought it was just you people over there doing
those terrible things to each other.

He closes the china cupboard. Her back is turned. She
mutters something at the metal vacuum tubes she's unclamp-
ing. He realizes he's finished his story anyway. Doesn't know
how to say the rest. She's humming, folding rags, stacking
them on the bottom pantry shelf. Lost in the cloud of her own
noise. Much more to his story, but she's not waiting around
to hear it. This is her last day before the holidays. He'd sealed
her bonus in an envelope, placed the envelope where he always does on the kitchen counter. The kitchen cabinet doors
have magnetic fasteners for a tight fit. After a volley of doors
clicking, she'll be gone. When he's alone preparing his evening meal, he depends on those clicks for company. He pushes
so they strike not too loud, not too soft. They punctuate the
silence, reassure him like the solid slamming of doors in big
sedans he used to ferry from customer to customer. How long
since he'd been behind the wheel of a car? Years, and now
another year almost gone. In every corner of the city they'd

be welcoming their Christ, their New Year with extravagant displays of joy. He thinks of Clara Jackson in the midst of her family. She's little but the others are brown and large, with lips like spoons for serving the sugary babble of their speech. He tries to picture them, eating and drinking, huge people crammed in a tiny, shabby room. Unimaginable, really. The faces of her relatives become his. Everyone's hair is thick and straight and black.

HOSTAGES

Her first husband, Ari, was darker than I am. Egyptian burnt toast with black beetle brows and sharp bones and hair tarry and straight as Geronimo's. I remembered him as fast and slick on the soccer field, a breakaway, one-on-one scorer with a rocket launcher of a foot. He played the game the way I imagined myself playing if I'd grown up in a soccer country, using my feet to catch and pass and shoot from distance, my feet as deadly as my hands that had learned their style on asphalt basketball courts in the city. Once I'd asked him about the constant fighting in the Middle East. He said he'd done his time in the Israeli army because all young men and women owed it. And said no, his squad had never been under fire, but close, and that was close enough for him. A black sky full of stars. The immensity of the open desert at night like a mirror so deep all those millions of stars got eaten and not a drop of light reflected from the sand. Close enough to know he never wanted closer to war than that field exercise near

the border, so close that you weren't permitted to talk or light
a cigarette after dark. A tomahawk of a face. All edges and
thin, stark bone skittish under mahogany skin. To me he was
the archetypal Arab, the swift bedouin horseman of the movies, so I was confused. Weren't Arabs enemies of the Jewish
state? Years later when I questioned her about his dark skin,
his accent, harsher, more guttural, more foreign than hers,
she said, Yes, an Arab . . . he was an Arab.

And my family nearly disowned me when I married him.
My mother hated Ari. Because he was irresponsible, she said.
But really because he was poor and dark, as dark as you
are. More eastern than European. A matter of class as much as
race. My relatives from the old country told me my grandmother would break into hives if Yiddish was spoken around
her. My mother barely escaped with her life from the Nazis.
But even that experience didn't convince her she was a Jew.
In Israel she remains a hostage, a queen in exile.

I hadn't seen her or her husband Ari for years so it was
like a ghost asking after ghosts. She'd emigrated permanently
from Israel, had another life, an American husband now. A
good man. Their son Eli had dribbled apple juice from his
bottle on my bare stomach as I bounced him on my knee. Her
son and husband, my wife and kids were having lunch in the
cottage. We'd stayed on the dock, enjoying the lake, a cloud-
less blue sky, the chance to reconnect. I'd asked about Ari
because I wanted to remind her I knew some of her history,
her loves and pain before this moment, this day we'd all
seemed to emerge bright and flushed from an amusement
park ride. Two couples and their children, families who'd
never seen each other as families before so there were a thousand ways of saying nothing. Kid stories, stale news of shared
acquaintances, endless chatty ways of squandering our chances

to say something by saying nothing. Till this moment when just the two of us are sitting alone, quiet, gazing at the calm surface of the water, light shows beyond the cove where wind fans the lake into shimmering pools and I questioned her about Ari and wondered what had become of him, of us, of the ten or twelve years since I'd wondered about anything just this way.

I love my life. I'm very lucky. When Eli's a little older, perhaps I'll look for a teaching job. To get out of the house. Michael's away all day. And I don't have many friends. The women where we've moved are impossible. They do nothing. Absolutely nothing all day. It would drive me crazy.

What would have happened if you'd taken me home to your parents?

She smiles. Not easy. It wouldn't have been easy.

Do you think Ari ever noticed anything?

He was too sure of himself to be jealous.

Too bad we never gave him something to be jealous about. Very, very jealous.

I remember trying.

No. You flirted, that's all. You were just as chicken as I was. You flirted.

And you flirted back.

I didn't know we were allowed to go further.

Such an innocent.

We were young. Just starting out our marriages. We didn't know any better.

Live and learn, eh. And what have you learned? Is it better to sneak around?

Damned if you do. Probably if you don't.

Has that made you unhappy?

Unhappy. Happy. Who cares? What's happy or unhappy

when things are as ugly as they are? The rich in a feeding
frenzy. The poor gearing up to fight one another for leftovers.
Race hate's respectable again.

She asks me how I can live here where people despise
me because of the color of my skin. I ask her where else
should I go? Would they love me in her old country?

How do you think Ari feels about the troubles on the
West Bank? Soldiers shooting Arab children daily.

She sighs: I don't know.

But he's there, isn't he? In Israel?

He's an Israeli.

I'm an American.

I hear the others returning. Twist in my seat.

Did you bring bread for the ducks?

A bagful.

Eli will love the ducks. That mother and her babies come
by every day. She started with ten. Down to seven little Indians now.

Every summer we see these strings of babies. About half
survive. Towards the end of August the little ones are as big
as the parents.

If you're still, they'll walk right up to your toes.

Yeah. You know they're really relaxed when they squat
and shit on the ramp. See all those white freckles?

I watch bread crumbs strike the water. The ripples. The
sallies of the birds. Their necks dart. A pecking order is maintained. Smallest last. They climb, half flying, half flutter and
jump, onto the ramp. Waddle up burlap matting towards us.
The mother remains in the lake, her yellow feet visible underwater, churning away. Seeing the busyness of her feet as she

sits serene in the water, it's as if I'm privy to a secret, that I know something about her she doesn't know I know.

Guerrillas have demanded the release of fifty freedom fighters within twenty-four hours or they will begin executing hostages, one an hour till all ten are dead. No official response to their demand has been announced at this time.

We discuss the crisis. Everyone in a lounge chair except my boys, who are digging in the sand off to the left on a tiny horseshoe of beach and Eli sitting behind us on a blanket with a few of their old toys. Ducklings settle into tufted, downy balls, tuck their heads into fluff, seven of them parked midway up the ramp. Eli squeals. The mother duck squawks her homing squawk, curve of her neck and head craned like a periscope as she rotates 360 degrees then rises in the water beating her wings. The whole brood kicks towards open water.

Eli had strayed off the blanket we'd spread to save his bare feet from the hot deck. He sobs, tries to climb back up her arms as she sets him down again on the blanket. She points to the gleaming, painted boards. Hot. Hot. Mimics jerking her finger back from a flame. Wiggles it. Blows on it. Hot. Hot.

Hostages are people held for ransom. Someone must pay something to preserve a hostage's life. Hostages are detained by force, ripped from one world, plunged into the limbo of another. Other human beings assume godlike power over the lives of hostages. Being a hostage is a little like dying and awaiting resurrection. Hostages are commodities, their humanity put on hold while they serve as chips in a power game;

they are also abstractions, symbols. Thus, the existence of hostages is paradoxically material and immaterial. Hostages are equally victims of those who love them and those who care nothing about them. Hostages are often blindfolded or beaten or stripped or raped to impress upon them their utter dependence and vulnerability, the absolute power of their captors. Sometimes hostages are displayed, photographed, paraded, videotaped, shown to be dupes, fools, proof of their captors' glory, the impotence of the violated.

Think of houses set miles back from sidewalks, jowly houses with green bibs of lawn tucked tight under their chins. Houses no one lives in. Because the streets are so wide and quiet. Yet shrubs, grass and enormous trees are too well groomed to be natural so someone must tend them, swarthy foreigners with loud machines and rattletrap pickups who descend regularly like locusts and then disappear without a trace except the brutal square-cornered neatness they leave behind. No one lives in the houses, at least not anyone like you know, unless you yourself reside in one of these suburban castles and even then you must have your doubts. Mirrors, polished surfaces of wood, tile, porcelain and stainless steel gleam not so much to receive your image as to devour it. The scale of walls and stairs and hallways oppresses you. Exotic, imported ornaments recall lost souls, passing as you do through the emptiness, insinuating that you are always a stranger in this monument built for gods.

Think of owning this residence, the equivalent of a circus tent in square feet enclosed under various hipped and cantilevered roofs that stamp the silhouette of your dwelling each night against the backdrop of burning sky. Think of a child

crying. A child's sleepscape shadowed by storm clouds till a
peal of thunder cracks the sky and a finger of light stabs down
to pluck out his eyes, pluck out his eyes. His first outcry is
sudden. Then you hear heartbroken sobbing. He's been un-
done that quickly by the dream. And you dry your hands on
a tea towel hanging by the kitchen sink, a towel pretending
to be grapes, strawberries, apples, bananas, cherries, the ever
ripe and perfect mood of bright fruit you chose to brighten
your kitchen. Oh love, you think, your empty womb pushed
up against teak cabinetry, squeezed there as if the room has
slammed shut behind you. Warmth spreads below your waist,
beginning and gone before you have a chance to acknowledge
it, the subtle guilt and expectation shooed away as baby
Eli weeps.

Think of being blindfolded. It's the price you pay for
being alive. You open your eyes each morning and a guillotine
crashes down, the dream ends. You are snatched into another
version of reality. One voted upon, certified and practiced by
consenting adults. You recognize your place in it as the fur-
niture of your room eases into view. Like starting up a novel
you closed the previous day, just before sleep. Nothing has
intervened. Characters take up midsentence where you've left
them when you grew drowsy and slipped under the covers and
reached up to twist off a lamp. The story is comfortable, a
page-turner. You know how it ends. But there are pages and
pages to go, a best-seller thicker than your mattress, your
fondest wishes.

Eli, Eli, darling. I'm coming, dear.

Your fingers are clean as a surgeon's. Why aren't they
stained by the colors of strangled fruit? Why do I hesitate,
staring at fingers as if I've never seen them before, one pale
hand drawing the other when Eli needs me? Grief is swarming

over him, dragging him back into that other world. His skull, his black bones shine through his skin.

He needs me. Why am I taking my time? Time that's not mine. Eli dear, will you still love me when I loom over your crib, my face bigger than the moon, my son, my stupid hands dropping into your bed, huge, awkward and dangerous as the weights at the end of chains wrecking the inner city whose ruins we must tour someday? Arm in arm, my son, we'll make a visit. I will be a frail, old lady with a hat tied under my chin. You will be my handsome Prince Charming. No one will wish us harm.

After he is diapered and fed and laid aside like a letter from someone at a great distance who is adored, she finishes as much as she remembers of what she was doing in the kitchen, then takes her spot at the upstairs window in the master bedroom. She recalls grooves scuffed inches deep into the granite floor of a guard post outside the gate of an ancient temple. She remembers her slow, rising horror—how many centuries, how many soft feet, how many hours shuffling and fretting had gouged these bruises and dents into the blackened stones. But she can't recall where she saw the footprints. Not in this infant nation. It must have been Greece or Turkey or Egypt or her own wounded country.

She finds herself asking other questions she can't answer. Which are more important, more *real*, omens or the events they portend. Today she believes it's omens. What happens, happens indiscriminately to everybody. The insult is universal, undistinguished. But the thrill, the dread of foreknowing rescues the seer from the numbing routine of events.

Tomorrow she'll fall on the other side of the argument. Events, with or without predictions, the steady day-by-day accumulation of the ordinary is what counts. Events without omens remain events, but what good are omens without the unraveling of what they predict?

But today she'll choose omens. Stirrings, presentiments in the cage of her skull. So what if nothing happens. So what if tomorrow comes or doesn't come. Omens have light and weight and spin. She relishes their luminous assurance that there's more to this life than meets the eye.

From the second-story window of the master bedroom she spies on black girls. Jamaican, Haitian, Puerto Rican, island girls in summer dresses, winter spring summer or fall. Colored girls in bright-colored dresses, rainbow blouses tucked into designer jeans. Emigrants like her. Women from warm countries who will always die a little when ice and snow cover this cold, adopted land. Their round, lively butts are balloons advertising themselves and the names of merchant princes. She envies the confidence of their buttocks. How do these maids, cooks, housecleaners and nannies afford designer jeans? Ari once described himself as *poor not cheap*, when she'd asked him why he'd spend money on a barber when she could trim his hair for him. She sees Ari wag his head, then grin and reach out to pat her hand, *poor not cheap*.

Is it Ari she's waiting for at the window this morning? Many mornings it was. Her Star. She called him that, *Star*, to tease him about his ambition to captain the national team, the six-pointed silver emblem he wore around his neck. He never grew older than the teenager he was when they first met in school. Slim and strong, like the boy Michelangelo discovered in a block of marble, only scrawnier, tougher, with a scrim of black hair webbing his dark skin. Ari running naked as a statue down the wide suburban sidewalks, his shadow bobbing on green lawns that reflect light in pools after automatic sprinklers spin their morning showers. Ari dressed like a cowboy strolling on the balls of his feet, ready to change pace or direction, hands poised above six-shooters crisscrossed low on his hips. Ari never troubles her broad street with its houses set back green miles from the curb except in her daydreams, her prophesies, and this morning at her post well before 9:00 A.M. with a whole day's shift still to pull, she isn't conjuring him, she's waiting for Eli's father to return in his purring German car.

Twenty minutes ago, twenty years ago she'd listened to the car, with her husband sealed inside, whine down the black strip of driveway, then roar into the gray street. He drives to the station, catches an early train to the city, leaves his sleek automobile with other sleek automobiles in the park-and-lock lot. She wishes he would invite her, just once, to ride with him to the station in the morning. She envies his car. She's jealous of its perfection, its sensuous leather upholstery, flashing digital lights. She'd crawl into the backseat after he boarded his train, tuck her legs under herself, doze through the day till another train brings him back. Like a pet. Like his faithful puppy automobile. All day long—heat or snow or rain—curled uncomplaining in the backseat. She'd enjoy weather against the roof. The rain's precise, military music. She'd be a piece of fruit ripening in a bell jar.

What if he forgot to retrieve her from those acres of expensive machines? Locked inside the car she'd shrivel like a raisin or turn to sticky, melted goo. Weeks later when he opens the driver's door, the putrid stench of her would em-

barrass him. Columns of sleek cars avert their eyes, turn up
their noses as he stands stunned, the perfectly engineered
handle in his hand. Guilt for a crime he didn't commit written
on his face, reflected in the sticky puddle that stinks so badly
his eyes water. Home again. Home again. She'd wait through
storm and sun, the tease of express trains that never stop.
She'll purr, she'll whine. Her doors will seal him safely in. Her
wipers dry his tears.

She remembers two of her dreams: girls playing in a huge,
manicured backyard. They are tickled by the coincidence of
their names, the fact each contains *Van*—Vanita, Van Tyne,
Vanessa, Vanna, Van de Meer, et cetera. They've just discovered this joke and it delights them, but very quickly the mood
shifts. Giggles cease, longer and longer gaps of silence. They
become aware of the size of the backyard. Its emptiness.
There's really no one else to talk to as the identities of the
group shrink to one girl. The silliness of the names is a mocking echo in her mind. The others have *van*ished. Far away,
trailing the squeal and thunder of an old-fashioned engine,
boxcars wobble along clickedy-click on toy wheels, like ducks
bobbing, wise old heads nodding, sucking on pipes, puffing
silent rings of smoke. She is weary and lonely. The jabbering
of her friends, the syllable *Van* they shared are part of the weight
this yard has accumulated. Its history bears down on her.

   If she doesn't awaken from this next dream she'll be
dead. But if she awakens, it will be two in the morning and
worse than death. She will blunder around in the darkness,
drink water, pop a pill, sit on the toilet. Sleep won't come
again for hours. Her heart thumps and sputters. Not enough
air. Her lungs ache. A bear scratches at the window. She's

alert now. Resigned, she lifts the covers and cool, merciful air infiltrates the clamminess beneath the blankets she steeples with her knees. A slab of icy hip beside her. Someone naked and dead in her bed. She is afraid to move. She knows it's her body lying next to her and the thought of touching it again paralyzes her. She's soaked in her own sweat. Thick as blood or paint. She can't see its color but knows it's dark. The color of her lover, a man whose sweat turns her to a tar baby too, wet and black and sticky. She will die if she moves, if she doesn't. If she opens her eyes, the iridescent clock will say 2:00 A.M.

Don't leave me this morning. Take me with you. Did the car ever make demands? Hang on him like one of these island girls with a dancer's ass, a witch's long, vermilion fingernails. Please take me. I can't bear to be alone today.

They wouldn't whimper it like that, would they? In their island babble she can't understand there would be better ways of saying *don't go*. Sometimes they were squirrels chattering. Squirrel talk. Squirrel brains. But if they wanted a man to stay with them, they'd put music in their voices. Blue music. Old blue songs learned from their grandmothers, the wrinkled ones with shopping bags who waited at the station, too. Past their prime, but still waiting, still dangerous. Terrorists hiding bombs in their bags. The black girls whisper in husky, fruity warbles. Stay and love me, baby. Don't go, darling. They'd twist the keys from his fingers and lead him up the carpeted stairs. They'd fuck all day, not notice her standing at the window wishing him back when he only left twenty minutes ago.

The Lamed-Vov are God's hostages. Without them humanity would suffocate in a single cry. She learned about them in a French novel that claimed they belong to ancient Talmudic legend. Lamed-Vov are sponges drawing mankind's suffering into themselves. She thought the dead photographer Diane Arbus might be one. A pampered rich girl escaping the suburbs, and wandering city streets, the city's misfits and lost ones her subjects—twins, midgets, corpses, derelicts, transvestites, giants, carny freaks, junkies, whores surrendering to her camera till the weight of it around her neck was too much and she slit her wrists and bled to death in the bathtub. According to the novel a thousand years is not long enough to thaw the agony each Lamed-Vov endures. When little Eli lay in an oxygen tent, racked by pneumonia, hollow-eyed, skeletal, too weak to cry or breathe or meet her eyes as she stared into his glass cage, she'd promised God that she'd be good, stop smoking, forfeit her life, do anything if her son was allowed to live. She begged the fever to leap from his chest to hers. The sneer, the nod dismissing, mocking her, was cold, cold. Why bargain if you held all the chips?

We have settled into the languor of a perfect Maine summer day. The loons were wild last night. Baying like dogs at the moon. They fractured sleep so it's easy to drowse away the day, sunbathing, cool dips in crisp lake water, then more sun and a few pages of a book, then more drowse. At about twelve we heard their car descending the gravel road behind our cottage. A new husband, new baby. It will be fun seeing her again. Meeting them.

〰

Guerrillas have demanded the release of one hundred freedom fighters within twenty-four hours or they will begin executing hostages, one an hour till all ten are dead. No official response to their demand has been announced at this time.

Are guerrillas devaluing the currency of guerrilla lives, admitting one enemy life is worth ten of theirs? Isn't this reverse discrimination? Isn't this equation just what their enemies have been asserting all along? Who's responsible for calculating such odds? Do children under twelve count as fractions of lives? Will some patriot volunteer a son or daughter if half a life is needed to make a deal come out even? Is it possible to bank hostages against future needs? A stockpile available for potential negotiations. If a hostage dies in transit, does he or she retain value? Can the body be turned in for credit? Is being a hostage any less a vocation than sainthood? Are hostages called or do they choose their calling?

Once, when I was a seed in my mother's womb, I overheard a gravelly voice threaten her with losing me if she didn't do exactly as the voice commanded. I'm here today telling the story so I must have survived, she must have paid.

In another version of the myth Adam weeps uncontrollably as Eve gives birth, a result neither had expected, another hostage in the garden.

Black girls have big teeth and laugh like squirrels. Their tails aren't bushy, but they're big, stamped with brand names like cattle. His dark three-piece suit for the next day hangs like a flayed skin in the closet behind her, which is larger than a room in most people's houses. If she turns from the window and walks into the closet and touches the suit, she will surely cry.

Black women seem fond of one another. They chatter endlessly. They touch one another constantly. Like her family's cook primped dough for the oven. She wishes they would talk to her but they fall silent when she approaches. Two of them are a crowd. Laughing, jostling, pulling faces, a choir of voices, astonished, pleased by each other, strangers, old, old comrades. If she didn't see them everyday after they finish their inside duties and take to the wide streets and the parklet at the end of the block with their white children, if she hadn't observed for hours from her solitary perch, she'd believe they were different girls each day and each day the new ones began fresh, innocent, reinventing those patterns, those intrigues she spied upon and registered in an empty book she thought she was saving for her own secrets.

One afternoon in a dark room with shades drawn they were watching home movies, forty-year-old flicks filmed before she was born when her husband was the chubby baby of his family. He's dressed for the occasion in a sunsuit remembered as blue. For these family follies, this gray-toned frolic aged like fine wine in a family vault with no other purpose than to preserve a day in time, a perfect prosperous day collected so everyone might see it and say Yes, life was like that, we smiled and mugged for the camera and yes isn't that a gorgeous automobile, yes, we had firm flesh, fine clothes, jewelry and fun long before there was a Jewish state and Arabs worrying its borders, Arabs with their damp jackal snouts prying into our secret lives, our vaults, our bright day in time when your husband was our boy-king tasty and plump as linen-covered basketsful of lunch lined up on a picnic table on the huge lawn of the huge house where he carried you forty years later across the threshold to meet us. She meets them again, the dead, the living, his family then and now in a funny paper of a movie after temple and a drive in the countryside.

She said she could tell me everything because I was black. Because I was black, I would understand.

She whispers into the shadows rippling across her husband's face. What year were these taken?

He whispers back, half of him still entranced by the dreamy action on the screen, I'm three . . . so it's 1943.

My mother was a prisoner then. In Auschwitz. I say the terrible word louder. *Auschwitz*. So I'm certain. Hope no one else overhears. Hope he understands. I don't want to spoil the party.

In one scene faces peer from a flat-topped touring sedan with a wire-spoked spare wheel inset behind the curl of its front fender. The photographer must be thinking of the circus in this shot. The magic car from which twenty clowns and a brace of dancing girls emerge, free at last after it wobbles down the midway. While the occupants are hidden from sight, nobody tattles, nobody lets out a peep. Then the cat springs from the bag. Joke's on everybody. A multitude stuffed like sardines in that tiny tin-can car with a calliope whistle. *Um pah. Um pah.* An astounded audience squeals as we unfold. That old circus scam is what the cinematographer must have had in mind as she sees his family packed in the car staring back at the camera.

She fears her husband might be hijacked on one of his business trips abroad. His grainy likeness appears on a tabloid's front page. He hasn't changed much. She recalls a sequence in the home movie. Or the movie triggers a flash-forward and she visualizes the kind of hostage he'd make. He's in a blue sunsuit, eating ice cream. He stops licking. A dreamy then blank, myopic stare held for a fraction of a second, long enough to register as a snapshot she glues in her secret, empty album. The picture's saved forty years. Long enough for the victim to be seen by millions. An exchange is being negotiated. She wonders how many dark lives must be sacrificed.

SURFICTION

Among my notes on the first section of Charles Chesnutt's
Deep Sleeper there are these remarks:

> Not reality but a culturally learned code—that is, out of the
> infinite number of ways one might apprehend, be conscious,
> be aware, a certain arbitrary pattern or finite set of indica-
> tors is sanctioned and over time becomes identical with re-
> ality. The signifier becomes the signified. For Chesnutt's
> contemporaries reality was *I* (eye) centered, the relationship
> between man and nature disjunctive rather than organic,
> time was chronological, linear, measured by man-made
> units—minutes, hours, days, months, etc. To capture this
> reality was then a rather mechanical procedure—a voice at
> the center of the story would begin to unravel reality: a
> catalog of sensuous detail, with the visual dominant, to in-
> dicate nature, *out there* in the form of clouds, birdsong, etc.
> A classical painting rendered according to the laws of per-
> spective, the convention of the window frame through which
> the passive spectator observes. The voice gains its authority

because it is literate, educated, perceptive, because it has aligned itself correctly with the frame, because it drops the cues, or elements of the code, methodically. The voice is reductive, as any code ultimately is; an implicit reinforcement occurs as the text elaborates itself through the voice: the voice gains authority because things are in order, the order gains authority because it is established by a voice we trust. For example the opening lines of *Deep Sleeper* ...

It was four o'clock on Sunday afternoon, in the month of July. The air had been hot and sultry, but a light, cool breeze had sprung up; and occasional cirrus clouds overspread the sun, and for a while subdued his fierceness. We were all out on the piazza—as the coolest place we could find—my wife, my sister-in-law and I. The only sounds that broke the Sabbath stillness were the hum of an occasional vagrant bumblebee, or the fragmentary song of a mockingbird in a neighboring elm ...

Rereading, I realize my *remarks* are a pastiche of received opinions from Barthes, certain cultural anthropologists and linguistically oriented critics and Russian formalists, and if I am beginning a story rather than an essay, the whole stew suggests the preoccupations of Borges or perhaps a footnote in Barthelme. Already I have managed to embed several texts within other texts, already a rather unstable mix of genres and disciplines and literary allusion. Perhaps for all of this, already a grim exhaustion of energy and possibility, readers fall away as if each word is a well-aimed bullet.

More Chesnutt. This time from the text of the story, a passage unremarked upon except that in the margin of the Xeroxed copy of the story I am copying this passage from, several penciled comments appear. I'll reproduce the entire discussion.

Latin: secundus-tertius-quartus-quintus.

"Tom's gran'daddy wuz name' Skundus," he began. "He had a brudder name' Tushus en' ernudder name' Squinchus." The old man paused a moment and gave his leg another hitch.

"drawing out Negroes"—custom in old south, new north, a constant in America. Ignorance of one kind delighting ignorance of another. Mask to mask. The real joke.

My sister-in-law was shaking with laughter. "What remarkable names!" she exclaimed. "Where in the world did they get them?"

Naming: plantation owner usurps privilege of family. Logos. Word made flesh. Power. Slaves named in order of appearance. Language masks joke. Latin opaque to blacks.

"Dem names wuz gun ter 'em by ole Marse Dugal' McAdoo, w'at I use' ter b'long ter, en' dey use' ter b'long ter. Marse Dugal' named all de babies w'at wuz bawn on de plantation. Dese young un's mammy wanted ter call 'em sump'n plain en' simple, like *Rastus* er *Caesar* er *George Wash'n'ton*, but ole Marse say no, he want all de niggers on his place ter hab diffe'nt names, so he kin tell 'em apart. He'd done use' up all de common names, so he had ter take sump'n else. Dem names he gun Skundus en' his brudders is Hebrew names en' wuz tuk out'n de Bible."

Note: last laugh. Blacks (mis)pronounce secundus. Secundus = Skundus. Black speech takes over—opaque to white—subverts original purpose of name. Language (black) makes joke. Skundus has new identity.

I distinguish remarks from footnotes. Footnotes clarify specifics; they answer simple questions. You can always tell

from a good footnote the question which it is answering. For
instance: *The Short Fiction of Charles W. Chesnutt*, edited by
Sylvia Lyons Render (Washington, DC: Howard University
Press, 1974), 47. Clearly someone wants to know, Where did
this come from? How might I find it? Tell me where to look.
OK. Whereas remarks, at least my remarks, the ones I take
the trouble to write out in my journal,* which is where the
first long cogitation appears/appeared [the ambiguity here is
not intentional but situational, not imposed for irony's sake
but necessary because the first long cogitation—*my remark*—
being referred to both *appears* in the sense that every time I
open my journal, as I did a few moments ago, as I am doing
NOW to check for myself and to exemplify for you the accu-
racy of my statement—the remark *appears* as it does/did just
now. (Now?) But the remark (original), if we switch to a different order of time, treating the text diachronically rather
than paradigmatically, the remark *appeared*; which poses another paradox. How language or words are both themselves
and *Others*, but not always. Because the negation implied by
appearance, the so-called "shadow within the rock," is *disappearance*. The reader correctly anticipates such an antiph-
ony or absence suggesting presence (shadow play) between the
text as realized and the text as shadow of its act. The dark
side paradoxically is the absence, the nullity, the white space
on the white page between the white words not stated but
implied. Forever], are more complicated.

The story, then, having escaped the brackets, can pro-
ceed. In this story, *Mine*, in which Chesnutt, replies to Chesnutt, remarks, comments, asides, allusions, footnotes, quotes
from Chesnutt have so far played a disproportionate role, and

Journal: unpaginated. In progress. Unpublished. Many hands.

if this sentence is any indication, continue to play a grotesquely unbalanced role, will roll on.

It is four o'clock on Sunday afternoon, in the month of July. The air has been hot and sultry, but a light, cool breeze has sprung up; and occasional cirrus clouds (?) overspread the sun, and for a while subdue his fierceness. We were all out on the piazza (stoop?)—as the coolest place we could find—my wife, my sister-in-law and I. The only sounds that break the Sabbath stillness are the hum of an occasional bumblebee, or the fragmentary song of a mockingbird in a neighboring elm ...

The reader should know now by certain unmistakable signs (codes) that a story is beginning. The stillness, the quiet of the afternoon tells us something is going to happen, that an event more dramatic than birdsong will rupture the static tableau. We expect, we know a payoff is forthcoming. We know this because we are put into the passive posture of readers or listeners (consumers) by the narrative unraveling of a reality which, because it is unfolding in time, slowly begins to take up our time and thus is obliged to give us something in return; the story enacts word by word, sentence by sentence in *real* time. Its moments will pass and our moments will pass simultaneously, hand in glove if you will. The literary, storytelling convention exacts this kind of relaxation or compliance or collaboration (conspiracy). Sentences slowly fade in, substituting fictive sensations for those which normally constitute our awareness. The shift into the fictional world is made easier because the conventions by which we identify the real world are conventions shared with and often learned from our experience with fictive reality. What we are accustomed to acknowledging as awareness is actually a culturally learned, contingent condensation of many potential awarenesses. In this culture—American, Western, twentieth century—an

awareness that is eye centered, disjunctive as opposed to or-
ganic, that responds to clock time, calendar time more than
biological cycles or seasons, that assumes nature is external,
acting on us rather than through us, that tames space by
manmade structures and with the *I* as center defines other
people and other things by the nature of their relationship to
the *I* rather than by the independent integrity of the order
they may represent.

An immanent experience is being prepared for, is being
framed. The experience will be real because the narrator pro-
duces his narration from the same set of conventions by which
we commonly detect reality—dates, buildings, relatives, the
noises of nature.

All goes swimmingly until a voice from the watermelon patch
intrudes. Recall the dialect reproduced above. Recall Kilroy's
phallic nose. Recall Earl and Cornbread, graffiti artists, their
spray-paint cans notorious from one end of the metropolis to
the other—from Society Hill to the Jungle, nothing safe from
them and the artists uncatchable until hubris leads them to
attempt the gleaming virgin flanks of a 747 parked on runway
N-16 at the Philadelphia International Airport. Recall your own
reflection in the fun house mirror and the moment of doubt
when you turn away and it turns away and you lose sight of
it and it naturally enough loses sight of you and you wonder
where it's going and where you're going and the wrinkly re-
flecting plate still is laughing behind your back at someone.

The reader here pauses　　　　　　Picks up in mid-

stream　a　totally　irrelevant
conversation:

... by accident twenty-seven double-columned pages by accident?

I mean it started that way

started yeah I can see starting curiosity whatever staring over somebody's shoulder or a letter maybe you think yours till you see not meant for you at all

I'm not trying to excuse just understand it was not premeditated your journal is your journal that's not why I mean I didn't forget your privacy or lose respect on purpose

it was just there and, well we seldom talk and I was desperate we haven't been going too well for a long time

and getting worse getting finished when shit like this comes down

I wanted to stop but I needed something from you more than you've been giving so when I saw it there I picked it up you understand not to read but because it was you you and holding it was all a part of you

you're breaking my heart

please don't dismiss

dismiss dismiss what I won't dismiss your prying how you defiled how you took advantage

don't try to make me a criminal the guilt I feel it I know right from wrong and accept whatever you need to lay on me but I had to do it   I was desperate for something, anything, even if the cost

was rifling my personal life searching through my guts for ammunition and did you get any did you learn anything you can use on me Shit I can't even remember the whole thing is a jumble I'm blocking it all out my own journal and I can't remember a word because it's not mine anymore

I'm sorry I knew I shouldn't as soon as I opened it I flashed on the Bergman movie the one where she reads his diary I flashed on how underhanded how evil a thing she was doing but I couldn't stop

A melodrama a god damned Swedish subtitled melodrama you're going to turn it around aren't you make it into

The reader can replay the tape at leisure. Can amplify or expand. There is plenty of blank space on the pages. A sin really given the scarcity of trees, the rapaciousness of paper companies in the forests which remain. The canny reader will not trouble him/herself trying to splice the tape to what came before or after. Although the canny reader would also be suspicious of the straightforward, absolute denial of relevance dismissing the tape.

Here is the main narrative again. In embryo. A professor of literature at a university in Wyoming (the only university in Wyoming) by coincidence is teaching two courses in which

are enrolled two students (one in each of the professor's sem-
inars) who are husband and wife. They both have red hair.
The male of the couple aspires to write novels and is writing
fast and furious a chapter a week his first novel in the professor's creative writing seminar. The other redhead, there are
only two redheads in the two classes, is taking the professor's
seminar in Afro-American literature, one of whose stars is
Charlie W. Chesnutt. It has come to the professor's attention
that both husband and wife are inveterate diary keepers, a
trait which like their red hair distinguishes them from the
professor's other eighteen students. Something old-fashioned,
charming about diaries, about this pair of hip graduate students keeping them. A desire to keep up with his contempo-
raries (almost wrote *peers* but that gets complicated real quick)
leads the professor, who is also a novelist, or as he prefers
novelist who is also a professor, occasionally to assemble large
piles of novels which he reads with bated breath. The novelist/
professor/reader bates his breath because he has never grown
out of the awful habit of feeling praise bestowed on someone
else lessens the praise which may find its way to him (he was
eldest of five children in a very poor family—not an excuse—
perhaps an extenuation—never enough to go around breeds
a fierce competitiveness and being for four years an only child
breeds a selfishness and ego-centeredness that is only exacer-
bated by the shocking arrival of contenders, rivals, lower than
dogshit pretenders to what is by divine right his). So he reads
the bait and nearly swoons when the genuinely good appears.
The relevance of this to the story is that occasionally the
professor reads systematically and because on this occasion
he is soon to appear on a panel at a neighboring university
(Colorado) discussing *Surfiction* his stack of novels was culled
from the latest, most hip, most avant-garde, new *Tel Quel* chic,

anti, non-novel bibliographies he could locate. He has determined at least three qualities of these novels. *One*—you can stack ten in the space required for two traditional novels. *Two*—they are *au rebours* the present concern for ecology since they sometimes include as few as no words at all on a page and often no more than seven. *Three*—without authors whose last names begin with *B*, surfiction might not exist. *B* for Beckett, Barth, Burroughs, Barthes, Borges, Brautigan, Barthelme . . . (Which list further discloses a startling coincidence or perhaps the making of a scandal—one man working both sides of the Atlantic as a writer and critic explaining and praising his fiction as he creates it: *Barth Barthes Barthelme.*)

The professor's reading of these thin (not necessarily a dig—thin pancakes, watches, women for instance are *à la mode*) novels suggests to him that there may be something to what they think they have their finger on. All he needs then is a local habitation and some names. Hence the redheaded couple. Hence their diaries. Hence the infinite layering of the fiction he will never write (which is the subject of the fiction which he will never write). Boy meets Prof. Prof reads boy's novel. Girl meets Prof. Prof meets girl in boy's novel. Learns her pubic hair is as fiery red as what she wears short and stylish, flouncing just above her shoulders. (Of course it's all fiction. The fiction. The encounters.) What's real is how quickly the layers build, how like a spring snow in Laramie the drifts cover and obscure silently.

Boy keeps diary. Girl meets diary. Girl falls out of love with diary (his), retreats to hers. The suspense builds. Chesnutt is read. A conference with Prof in which she begins analyzing the multilayered short story *Deep Sleeper* but ends in tears reading from a diary (his? hers?). The professor recognizes her sincere compassion for the downtrodden (of which in one of his fictions he is one). He also recognizes a fiction in her husband's fiction (when he undresses her) and reads her diary. Which she has done previously (read her husband's). Forever.

The plot breaks down. It was supposed to break down. The characters disintegrate. Whoever claimed they were whole in the first place? The stability of the narrative voice is displaced into a thousand distracted madmen screaming in the dim corridors of literary history. Whoever insisted it should be more ambitious? The train doesn't stop here. Mistah Kurtz he dead. Godot ain't coming. Ecce Homo. Dat's all, folks. Sadness.

And so it goes.

ROCK RIVER

Main Street out of Rock River narrows abruptly into a two-lane and in twenty-five minutes you are in the middle of nowhere. Past a couple clumps of buildings that used to be towns and one that might still be, then a railroad embankment's on your left for a while till it veers off over the plains, a spine of mountains to the right, blue in the distance, miles of weather-cracked wasteland stretching to foothills hunkered like a pack of gray dogs at the base of the mountains. Moonscape till you turn off at the Bar H gate on the dirt track under the power line and follow it through a pass, along a ridge and then things get brown, green some, not exactly a welcome mat rolled out but country you could deal with, as long as you don't decide to stay. Trees can tunnel out of thickets of boulders, grass can root in sand and shale, the river you can't find most summers in its seamed bed manages to irrigate a row of dwarf cottonwoods whose tops, situated as they are, higher than anything else around, black-green sil-

houettes orderly on the horizon, remind you that even the
huge sky gives way to something, sometimes, that its weight
can be accommodated by this hard ground, that the rooster
tail of dust behind your pickup will dissipate, rise and settle.

The road twists and bumps and climbs, curves back on
itself, almost disappears totally in a circus of ruts, gouges and
tire-size stones, dropping steadily while it does whatever else
it's doing, shaking the pickup to pieces, steering it, tossing it
up and catching it like a kid warming up a baseball. No seat
belt and your head would squash on the roof of the cab. Last
few miles the steepest. Then this fold of land levels, meadows
and thick, pine woods, sudden outcroppings of aspen, hillocks,
miniravines, deer country, a greenness and sweet smell of water cutting the sage, a place nothing most of the trip here
would have suggested you'd find.

I am alone. My job is to clean up Rick's truck, get it
ready to bring back to town. They said that would be all right
now. The police have finished their investigation. Tomorrow
I'll come back with Stevenson. He can drive my truck and I'll
drive Rick's. But today I want to do what I have to do by
myself. I expect it will be a mess. He stood outside, but the
blast carried backwards to the open window of the truck. They
warned me, then they said the gas is OK. Better take jumper
cables, though, Quinson said. As if any fool wouldn't know
that. Cops were making arrangements to tow it to town. I
thought I'd rather drive it. Clean it up first. Then me and
Stevenson come out and I'll bring it in.

I have old towels. Two five-gallon cans of water. Upholstery cleaner. Brillo. Spot remover. Mr. Clean, sponges, rags,
Windex, all the tools on my knife, heavier gear like shovel, ax
and rope that's always stowed in the truck box. I think I have
enough. Mary Ellen said, Take this, holding out a can of Pine-

Sol spray deodorant. I hadn't thought of that and was surprised she did and didn't know what to say when she held it
out to me.

I shook my head no, but she didn't take it back. Didn't
push it on me but she didn't pull it away either.

I think to myself. Can't hurt, can it? There's room. So I
took it.

She nodded. Rick got on her nerves. He liked her. He
reminded her of her father. Hopeless. Hopeless. Hopeless. You
had to smile and be nice to him he was so hopeless. She'd
never neglect the small kindnesses to him she said because
you'd never want him to feel you'd given up on him. But he
could try your patience. Try a saint's. He couldn't count the
times she'd said in private she'd given up on Rick. Don't
bring him around here anymore, she'd say. I'm sick and tired
of that man, she'd say. But then she'd always hug Rick or cry
on his shoulder or say something awful and provoking to let
him know she was very well aware of how hopeless he was,
and let him know he'd never force her to give up on him.

Mary Ellen.

It's been a week. They probably locked it and shut the
windows to keep out the rain. They'd want to protect a brand-
new vehicle like that.

Almost new.

Looked new. He was so cockeyed proud of it.

I doubt Sarah will want to keep it. Either way if it's
cleaned up, that's one thing she won't have to bother with.

Will you be all right?

There's room. Won't hurt to take it. They probably did
close up the windows.

I have Rick's extra set of keys. Went by his house to get
them. Here's what I saw.

A tall woman. Sarah, Rick's wife. In blue jeans sitting at
a table with a look I'd seen somewhere before, a picture of a
Sioux Indian in a long line of Indians staring at the camera
and it was hard to tell whether male or female, the photo was
old and brown, the face I remembered round and the hood
of dark hair could be a woman or a long-haired Indian man.

Sarah never wore blue jeans. Dresses almost always. If
pants, they were slacks with sewn-in creases. You could never
guess what she might say or do but her clothes wasn't the
place that she showed she was diffcrent. I liked her a whole
lot less than I liked Rick. Nobody talked more than Rick once
he'd had his few drinks but you knew Rick didn't mean anything by it. When Rick talked you could tell he was talking
just to keep himself from sinking down. If he stopped talking,
he'd be in trouble, worse trouble than anything he might say
would get him in. He needed to keep talking so he could sit
there with you and play liar's poker or watch a campfire burn
or just drink on Friday afternoon at the Redbird where we all
did to forget the week that was. He'd make people mad who
didn't know him because he was subject to say anything about
anybody, but after a while, if you were around Rick any
amount of time at all you knew it was foolish to take what he
said seriously, personally. Rick was just riding along on this
stream of words, merrily, merrily riding along and you could
ride it too or pay it no mind, cause he wasn't really either.

Sarah on the other hand couldn't be any way but personal. She couldn't say Howdy-do without an edge to it. Like
she's reminding you she had spoke first, giving you a lesson
in manners and too bad you weren't raised right. I think the
woman just couldn't help it. Something about growing up in

too holy a house. Like the best anybody could do would never be good enough. And somebody had to take the job of reminding people of that fact. So here's Sarah. Eagle eyed and cat quick to pounce on universal slovenliness and your particular personal peccadilloes any hour of night or day. In blue jeans. Looking, as you might suspect, as if she's sleeping poorly or not at all, on the losing side force-marched by cavalry back to the reservation and mug shot. A drink on the kitchen table and offering me one even though we both know it's barely ten o'clock in the morning and that's not what I came for, reminding me, her lips pursed tight, that I'm in no position to judge her, in fact just the opposite case, because when she stares up at me red eyed there's just a little silliness, a little judgmentalness, a little I-know-better-than-you this is not the right thing to be doing but we've both started drinking earlier of a morning, you many more mornings than I, and you with Rick nonstop so morning, afternoon or night left far behind.

I better not stop now.

Didn't think you would.

Better get this done while I'm feeling up to it.

Why don't you let the police handle it?

It's just something I thought I could do. Ease a little of the burden.

You've done enough already. We're all grateful for what you've done for us.

They were going to tow it. Makes more sense to drive it. They said if it was all right with you, it was all right with them. I'm happy to help out if it's OK with you.

There the keys are on the table.

I won't be bringing it back today. Thought I'd just go up today and see what had to be done. Get it ready and tomorrow Stevenson said he would ride up with me and drive my truck back.

Don't bring it here.

You want me to park it at my place?

I don't care where you park it. It's Rick's truck. He won't be needing it. His brains were all over the seat. He drove away from us in that cute little shiny red truck and I don't care if I never see it again.

It's almost new. Rick talked himself up on a real bargain. Probably get most of what he paid if you sell it.

You've been a great help. Keep the truck. He'd want you to have it.

I couldn't do that.

I have some other stuff of his you might want as well. To remember him by. You can have his shotgun if the cops return it.

If you want me to take care of selling the truck I'd be happy to try. I'm sure it will bring a good price. From the outside it seemed in decent shape. Police sealed it and roped off the clearing where it was parked but as far as I could tell from where they kept us standing, everything was fine. Quinson told me it has plenty of gas, that I should bring cables just in case. I guess he thought I was born yesterday.

Simon?

Yes.

Do you miss him?

I'm real sorry. My heart goes out to you and your fine boys.

I can't miss him. He was gone too long.

Still in a state of shock, I guess. I sat there at the funeral still hoping Rick would change his mind.

He left while I was sleeping. I didn't get worried till the

third day. I woke up early, early that morning and decided
I'd call you. Ask if you'd seen him. Begin the whole humili-
ating routine. Has anybody seen my husband wandering
around town? Blue eyes, blond, slightly balding, eyeglasses,
middle-aged but boyish face, till he's acutely sloshed, then he
resembles his grandfather's corpse. Tame when sober, answers
to the name Rick. Please call 545-6217 if you've seen this
individual. No reward. Except knowing you've saved a happy
home. I'd made up my mind to begin phoning around and
you of course were at the top of the list, but the cops called
me first.

What I saw was she looked like parts of this town, skimpy
as it is, I haven't seen for years. Below Second Street, near
the railroad tracks where there are storage bins for rent. It's
a ragtag, helter-skelter whole lot of nothing dead end. Nobody
lives there. Nobody's ever going to or ever has. You can hear
sixteen-wheelers humping on the interstate, trains rattle across
the overpass. It's the kind of hardscrabble little patch of con-
crete and gravel and cinders and corrugated tin-roofed sheds
that will always be at the edge of towns on the prairie and
outlast the rest—downtown, the nice neighborhoods—be here
when no one's left to listen to coyotes howling, the sage
running, wind at night screaming in as many voices as
there's stars.

What I saw was her eyes on a level only slightly below
mine, fixing me, daring me to ignore them. The last party at
their house is what I saw. Rick was chef. Spaghetti sauce from
ground antelope. Elk liver pâté. Neatly wrapped packages from
his game locker that I'd seen thawing, blooding in his refrig-
erator when I'd popped in for a Bud the afternoon before.
Sarah's eyes told me Rick probably hadn't been to bed or
stopped drinking before he started up for this party. He'd

been telling the story of how he'd tracked the wily elk whose
liver was being nibbled as an hors d'oeuvre on Ritz crackers.
No one was listening so Rick was telling it softly, slouched
down in an armchair, telling again what he'd related at least
three times to every single one of us that evening, mumbled
quietly, one more time, his gestures slow motion as somebody
underwater, his eyes invisible behind his bifocals, his drink
glass abiding on the chair's mashed-potato arm, sunken as
deeply, as permanent as Rick is in its lap. You pass by and
think that man's not moving soon, nor his drink, and wonder
how they ended up that way and wonder if they'd ever get
unstuck from the tacky fruit-and-flower print slipcover that
couldn't hide the fact that easy chair had seen better days.

Eye to eye with Sarah and she winks at me, even though
both of us long past having fun at this party. But she's sloshed
and I'm two sheets and that's why we both came so I wink
back and hear the banjo and fiddle and whiny hill voices from
the next room, the slapping of knees, whooping and stomping.
It's getting good to itself in there. Dancing usually means wee
hours before you can squeeze everybody out the door. It's
what we've come for. To stay late. To holler a little bit and
grab ass and thump a little on one another. I look back but
Sarah's gray eyes are gone in the direction of the music, but
music's not what's in them. I know by the set of her jaw
what's in them. If I was close enough so her breath would
ripple my lashes, that close but invisible so I wouldn't spoil
her view, what I'd see would be two little Ricks, one in each
gray globe of her eyes, two Ricks the stereo in her brain turns
to one in three dimensions, real as things get in a kitchen at
11:00 P.M. when a full-scale party's raging.

Sure enough what I see is him stumbling into the kitchen
this morning, hitting both sides of the doorframe before he

gets through. He tries one more step. More lurch than step. As if his dancing partner has fooled him. He reaches for her hand and she whirls away laughing and he's caught with his weight on the wrong foot and almost falls on his nose after her. But he respects the quickness, the cunning, the spinning sexy grace in her, and forgives and catches himself with a little clumsy half skip, half shuffle, do-si-do, it's just a thing that happens. Hi. Hi. Hi. All. He catches me red-handed sliding the keys off the vinyl tablecloth. There are too many to close in my fist. She didn't separate the truck keys from the rest, twelve, thirteen, fifteen keys in my fist. I could shake them and make a mighty noise, shake them to the beat of that dancing music from the next room.

Where you going with ma keys, Simon? Simon-Simon. What you doing wit ma fucking keys, boyo? Ho. Ho. Don't touch that dial.

He glides in slow. The tempo has changed. He clamps one hand on Sarah's shoulder. Twirls her so she lands smack up against his chest. Then they are both gliding cheek to cheek and the song is waltz time, but they two-step it, hitch around the kitchen graceful as Arthur Murray and Ginger Rogers on stilts. Don't stop when Rick's elbow chops a whole row of empty beer bottles off the counter and they tumble and break and scatter and the worst godawful racket in the world does not attract one interested or curious face from the party in the other room.

WHEN IT'S TIME TO GO

Peace, my brother. Those hills on the horizon give up the golden light and we won't have it to worry about no more. I'm just as tired as you are. I know it's late. But sleep's like pussy. And pussy like meat on the bone. You can worry it or leave it alone. So don't you go yet, brother. Hold on least till I finish my story.

I click my glass on his and he starts.

Once upon a time was this little blind boy. He lived in Alabam boom bang a langa. His mama was named Clara and his daddy one those no-name shadows drop like a icy overcoat on you when you ain't looking. You be standing in the sun, happy as a tick on a bloody bug all the sudden it's black as night and you shivering like cold's a knife slicing your liver. Why? Cause that shadow got you. Done dropped out of no-where and got you good, that's why. Little boy's daddy was a shadow like that and he told Clara he loved her and gave her a baby behind him swearing how beautiful she was and how

much he loved her and rubbing her big butt and telling her
he'd stay with her always. Well, he came up a little short on
the always. Had him a young girl the whole time Clara carrying his son and woulda been long gone before the little bun
popped out the oven if Clara hadn't turned him to a stone, a
stone black as pitch-black night and cold as white people's
lies. So the little blind boy, little Sambo was born with magic
on one side and night on the other. No wonder there was a
caul over his head. It turned him blue, just about strangled
him. They buried it under a tree so it wouldn't come back
like a sneaky cat trying to steal his breath.

Well, it wasn't long before the lil fella could talk. Chatter
like a treeful of ravens and the lil thing ain't no bigger than
a minute, ain't nine months old and got a mouth on him tell
you more than you care to know. Folks could see from the
beginning he was something special. Look what his mama was.
Look who they think was his daddy. And look at the shopping
bag he came here in. And them eyes. Them long eyes look
right through you but can't see a thing. Some say they was
green and some say they was lavender. Some say you could
hear that child's eyes crackle you get close enough. Like the
dust cooking on a light bulb some people swore they heard it
and that's what the sound was. Or a moth circling something
hot that's gon kill it sooner or later.

Was a time he could see just like you or me. Born blind
but after a while you wave something in front his eyes they'd
follow it back and forth, back and forth so you knew he knew
something was there. Got so he would reach out his hand and
find what you was dangling. Like keys, or a watch, or a ear-
ring, whatever shiny a person shake at him to catch his eyes.
He got better and better and we thought Praise the Lord he's
gon have eyes like the rest us.

So once upon a time he could see the light. Least we thought he could. That's a blessing cause how you spozed to tell anybody been in dark all they life about sunshine? How you gon say red or green or blue if all they know is the black black at the heart of black? So he knew about light, about mist in the morning, and sparrows breaking across a blue sky and leaves turning and all the colors niggers be wearing in they skins. Which depending on how you see it is better or worse once the light start to failing. I mean maybe you don't miss what you never had. Maybe never having nothing is a blessing in disguise. On the other hand if you seen the light once, then you got it inside where can't nobody take it. Even if somebody steal it from the world and it's gone forever you got that memory. You got it to fall back on don't matter they bury you ten miles underground and stack another mile of rocks on top you still got the memory down there in that black hole with you.

He was round about nine or ten when it start happening again. When the dark start closing in again. He said, Mama, the hills keep getting closer. I sits still but the hills keep sliding closer, picking up speed, getting taller and wider and the green trees covering them black as tar. Moving towards him fast as his daddy moves away in his dream. His dream of a father striding bandy-legged faster and faster, kicking up dust in the twisting road till he ain't nothing but a speck and a feather of smoke.

They couldn't go to the doctor treated only white folks and the one treated anybody he got that whiskey on his breath and them yellow-cake teeth people got to turn they face away and he's thinking like it's respect or some dumb scared rabbit coons fraid to look him in the eye. Ol Mr. Shitbreath Doctor, he don't know squat. Say: Peel that crust in the morning. Say: Hot rags, hot as he can stand, and peel that crust away.

His mama Clara listens, stares down at her bad feet in tennis sneakers with open toes so her corns can breathe. If her feet wasn't hurting so bad this morning she'd stomp a hole in the nasty floor. She can see where somebody skimmed a mop through the dirt. Like somebody grabbed the ankles of his skinny nurse and turned her upside-down and dragged her witchy hair across the linoleum. Stomp a hole clean through and let the whole dirty office slide back where it came from. Let the white table and his squeaky spinning stool and pills and bottles and needles and sticks and those rubber gloves he rolls on to stick his finger up your ass, let it all gurgle down the hole like dishwater draining out the sink.

Got to peel it, baby. I know it hurts but I got to get it all off.

Some call Clara a witch. They remember Clyde McDonald spinning like a roach what got that Kills-em-Dead all over his eight feet, spinning like a crazy top and roaring like he's on fire till he dropped dead in front of Minnie Washington's porch and Min she just sitting there rocking, rocking and watching him spin faster and faster till he bright as a light bulb about to pop, till he did pop and laid there curled dead as the dust at her feet. Told you so, Min said. She fixed him sure enough. Min the one sicced Clara on his trifling behind and told everybody she did it and would do it again, a thousand times again he hurt her so bad he ain't nothing but a dog and a coward and a baby-killing rat. Min never said hello or good-bye to Clyde McDonald just watched him spinning and watched him drop and ain't never missed a beat in her rocker. So people knew Clara was a witch. Much witch as she wanted to be even though it was a long time ago she did that

business for Min. Some the younger sassy ones asking if Clara
so bad why don't she cure her blind child her own bad self.
Why she trotting way down the road to that whiskey-head
quack she so bad. Well, there's some people you can't tell
nothing to anyway. Mize well save your breath cause ignorant's the way they born, the way they gon stay till the day
they die. Ain't no sense trying to tell them nothing so you just
shake your head and remember Clyde spinning through the
dust. It's more than one kind of power in the world. Ain't no
kind of power can win all the time. If one thing don't work
don't be too proud to try something else. Clara loved her boy.
Maybe she loved him so much she touch him and ain't no
magic in her hands ain't nothing but a natural woman when
she touch him cause she love him so much.

Be that as it may the light steady failing her boy. Thick
crust over his eyes every morning. Like the hills and the trees
sneaking up on him at night, like they creeping closer all the
time and he's always picking pieces of tree and dirt and dark
off his eyelids. Getting closer every day. The place they call
the horizon, where the sky stops being sky, where the edges
of sky and ground make one long seam, that place is closing
down like a scar over a wound.

Sambo wrings them boiling rags and lays them on his
eyes. Hot as he can stand it, hot enough to suck all the color
out his skin, so it's bleached like side meat been cooking all
day. He a tough little monkey and scared too so he lays them
on hot as he can stand it. Thinks of fire. Thinks he got to
burn to see. His eyeballs burning like they up there in the
sky, in the fire colors of sunset. He sits blind as a bat with
them hot pads over his eyes and tries to think of things take
his mind off the scalding, till the crust gets soft and sticky
like candy. He sees the world turning, crackling like a piece

of fish in a frying pan when you flip it over. One side brown
and crispy, the other white as a ghost. He remembers the good
times before he got here. Swimming round. Kicking his legs
like a frog. Everything mellow like it is when you dive deep
in the river and squeeze your eyes tight shut. He thinks if I
do it right this time, if I push back the dark far enough this
time, won't be crowding me tomorrow.

But he knows better. His mama told him better. Said the
light's failing. Said it be worser and worser fore it get better.
Nothing we can do but try to hold on to the little light you
got. Fight for it every morning. Get them rags hot as you can
stand it and fight that crust.

Sambo a good boy. Don't never sass. Always listen to his
mama so he fought it every morning like she say. But one
morning he got to dreaming behind those rags. Got to dreaming cause it's better than hurting and it was a dream he told
his mama later, a dream of shedding them rags and getting
up off his bed and walking out the door and starting down
the road towards the hills where the sun rises every day God
sends. He walks in his dream and the rags is gone and the
fire is gone and he just goes about his business counting
everything he sees. Trees, birds, squirrels, chipmunks and
whatnot scooting and crawling through the weeds. Counts ants
and blades of grass. Not missing a thing and counting everything at once cause that light feels so good, so easy and cool
in his dream. Like the swimming time, the paddling time.
Light carries him along. *Singing* is how he told it. Light was
just singing to me, Mama, and telling me I didn't need no
eyes. Wasn't no such a thing as eyes less you call your knees
and hands and shoulders eyes cause everything you got can
hear the light, or touch it and everything you got is something
to see with. Told her it was a dream but then other folks said,

I seen your boy, Clara. Sure was in a hurry to get somewhere, the other morning. Must be all better now, ain't he? Walking and whistling by, ain't never said howdy-do, good morning or good-bye, but he was steady trucking somewhere.

And that's the kinda thing make his mama scared. Cause she was a witch and knew about power and knew about turning to air, about rushing through your own bones, about running like sweet marrow and leaving your bones hollow as a reed. About being in two places at once. So you can mind your mama, so you can lay on your bed with hot rags on your eyes and at the same time, be running round the countryside. Dreaming one place while you supposed to be in another and the power lets you be in both. One man can watch you snoring and another swear you was in his henhouse stealing eggs. Clara scared cause if the boy had power, he had to pay the piper. And the piper kept her lonely and a fool all the days of her life. Made her wrap her legs round his daddy and holler hallelujah. Made her bow down when he reared up over her. Made her be mare to his stallion when it shoulda been her riding him till wasn't nothing left but bloody nubs where his arms and legs supposed to be.

Yeah, they might could have saved my sight. Ain't never gon forgive them that. Number-one cracker didn't treat colored so wasn't nowhere else to go but down the road to the whiskey head that did. My mama took off work one morning and carried me down there but the old bad-breath turkey couldn't do no good. So here I sit behind these shades blind as a rock.

Must have been twelve or thirteen years old when I left home. Gripping the handles of my shopping bag so tight it put a crease in my hand I can feel today. Tear my whole arm out the socket only way you get that bag with everything I

owned away from me. Mama told the bus driver. Leave him
be. Let him find the steps his ownself. Mama was like that.
Had to be. Other folks treat me like I was blind but she know
better. She the one let me fall on my face. Let me slam my
shins, ride my bike, let me cross the road by myself and walk
on down to the store. She said if he don't do it hisself, he
ain't never gon learn. Be crippled for sure if he always waiting
till somebody else do for him.

So I was steady gripping my shopping bag and listening
at that bus motor humming. There's a place where the door
be breathing. You know. A place like a mouth where the
inside air leaving and outside air pushing in and it's warmer,
it's got a different smell, that's how you find a open door.
Motor sound tells me it's a big bus so I know I got to step
up on it but I don't get situated quite right and bang my
ankle and I'm seeing fire and gripping my bag and thinking,
Shit, I can't even step up in this damn bus how I'ma get
around when it stop a thousand miles away in some damn
place I never been before. But I hear Mama say, Leave him
be, Mr. Driver. He'll find it all right.

And you know I been bumping my shins and tripping
over things and falling flat on my face ever since but I ain't
never considered turning back. Ain't never felt sorry for myself neither cause my mama never did and I know she love
me better than I love my ownself.

That's what little Sambo said, a grown man sitting on a
barstool in the Crawford Grill in the Hill District in Pitts-
burgh, Pennsylvania. How do I know that? Well, I was on
another stool and it was after the last set and the bartender
had locked the door so it was just us and quiet. Us locked in
and everybody else locked out while Raymond the bartender
went about his business closing down the bar. Just Raymond

and me and Sambo and Marylou, the waitress, cleaning off
the booths and tables. Just her shuffling slow-motion on tired
feet and the tinkle of glasses gathered, washed, stacked. Raymond humming a low-down bluesy something while he wipes
and stashes things away. Nobody exactly a stranger to nobody.
You know. We all just out there at the end of the night, in
the early morning if the truth be told, out there after most
people have gone about their business, home sleeping in their
beds if they got good sense, but we're holding on, holding out
after the music's over and the night's over and in a hour or
two if we keep on hanging on it's light when you step outside.
So what you are saying you sort of say to anybody who cares
to listen because you're saying it mostly to yourself. Hey. You
know what I mean. You been there, ain't you, sisters and
brothers. In the Crawford Grill at three-thirty in the morning
on barstools rapping.

Sambo talking slow and easy as molasses. Yeah. Left the
country with everything I had in a shopping bag. Didn't know
where in hell I was going. New Orleans nothing but a name
to me. But I knew I could play. Knew they had pianos in New
Orleans and if I could find me one and sit down and get my
fingers on them keys, somebody would listen.

Been on the road ever since. Finding pianos and playing
and paying my way. One place get just the same as another
afterwhile. Be worse if I had eyes. When you got eyes it's too
easy to forget. I mean you can get around and don't have to
pay attention to nothing. Eyes get to be like them dogs lead
blind people around. They do the seeing and you just follow
along behind. You forget the light. You steady losing the light
and don't even know it's gone.

So that's about all of it, my friends. Sambo could sure
nuff play. I'm a witness. Yes I am. Point of the story, I guess,

if it has one, I guess, if it got to, is look down at your hands. Look at the blood in the ropes in the backs of your hands. Think of that blood leaving you and running up in somebody else's arms, down into somebody's fingers black or brown or ivory just like yours. And listen to those hands playing music. Now shut your eyes. Shut them for good. And ask yourself if anything's been lost, if something's been taken away or something given. Then try to remember the color of light.

CONCERT

Death drapes the stage like all those things you know you must do when the performance is over.

Buck called.

Your mother, man. It's your mother ...

Shit, Buck. Don't say it. Buck your magic twanger.

Everybody in the auditorium on their feet now. Putting their hands together. You'll catch the first fast train out of here. The piano man and bass player wink, nod and mouth words at each other like lovers across a crowded room. You hear again the groan of him slicing the bow across the fat belly of the bass. Screeching halt. A trolley stop when the treacly ballad threatened to la-di-da forever and with one throaty gasp, one pen stroke the bassist ended it. One man, one vote. Everybody out. You consider the formality of their dress. Tux. Black tie. How the starched white shirtfronts sever their dark heads. Cannonballs dropped in the snow. You commiserate. Monkey suits. Monkeyshines. How many one-night stands in front of all these strangers. Who listen. Who applaud. What. Inside the elevator of their music. Going up. Down. The brothers too smooth to move. Wearing refrigerators. Laid out ice elegant on cooling boards. Got a letter this morning, how do you reckon it read? How do you reckon it read? That letter. This morning.

Can you hear me? Lots of static on the line. I can barely . . .

Why are they costumed as pallbearers? Why the morticians' manners? Have they been pulling legs so long they don't have one left to stand on? You think of Africans down on their knees scrabbling for grains of wheat dribbling from gunnysacks slabbed on a U.N. relief truck. You imagine those skeletons inside these formal suits. The high-butt shuffle of the xylophone man tells you which corner and which year and which city he hails from. Surely as the zebra's wobbly gait in his zoo pen recalls haul-assing across a Serengeti plain. The thinnest note's too heavy for these African ghosts to bear. They shiver in the shivering heat and expire. You are left alone shimmering till he bops the metal plate again. Bell ringer. Stinger. Big Bopper. Word Dropper. Quells the vibrations with his padded mallet.

One last tune. From our latest album. Available now at your record store. That was, by the way, a commercial, ha, ha. A composition we've entitled . . .

Buck, Buck.

It's ten here. Two hours difference.

If I hurry home, it won't have happened yet.

Do you remember driving into the City? From Philly over the bridges into Jersey. Flat out up the pike then the tunnel. Didn't it seem everybody going our way, headed for the same place? All those cars and trucks and buses, man.

Planes in the air. Trains. Close to Newark you could even see
ocean liners. Every damn form of transportation known to
man, man. And every kind of high. All making it to the City.
Unanimous. The people's choice. And you were there in that
number. Doing it, boy. Shoom. Kicking the Jersey turnpike.
Pedal to the metal. Radio already there and sending back
waves. Chasing. Chased. Won't it be something when all these
folks pour down through the tunnel and we're each and all of
us packed into the same tight squeeze of our destination. The
Five Spot. Lintons. The Village Gate. Miracle of planes trains
buses cars ships arriving and checking in and checking out
the scene. I can't wait. Nobody can. Ghosts boogie through
the marshes. A nasty KKK greeting scrawled in four-foot-tall
letters on an overpass. We see city lights braced for us. A line
of hostiles on the horizon deciding whether they'll let us pass
or swoop down and burn the wagons. How long ago was that,
Buck? I haven't forgotten any of it. Not that long ago, really.
I was in college, first in my family, first splib this and that,
the early sixties first time I checked these guys out. Now the
bass player's head is bowed, his eyes closed. Is he remembering my dream? Piano man, bottom lip belled, sputters like a
trumpet as he gazes down at the intricate journeying of his
long fingers. I notice the bass man's hair is thinning, even
worse than mine, over the crown of his skull. Brown skin
dropped over his eyes blinds him. Two sightless bubbles trans-
fix the audience. When he can't sleep he counts the fences
his four fingers have jumped over, his dangling thumb along
for the ride. Oh, it's a long way from May to December. So
willow. Willow weep for me. I think *Ashanti* describes the bass
man because the word sounds spare, sparse, taut. Quiver attached to the fiddle holds an arrow he will shoot into someone's heart. Wheels turning behind his blind eyes choose the

victim. *Ashanti* because he's a warrior. Hard. Pitiless. His eyes
rolled back into his skull. Madness. Ecstasy. The blank mask
surveys us. Choosing a target. Nothing reveals what the hidden eyes think of us yet we know our measure is being taken,
know that part of us begs to be seen by someone else in order
to be real. We're in mortal danger if no mirror remembers
us, reminds us what to do next.

Buck. Buck.

Listen, man. I got something important to tell you. Your
mother, man.

Wait. Let me tell you this dream I've been scoping lately.
See, you call me on the phone. I'm sitting in a theater. Not
a movie theater. A theater theater. Phone rings. I'm aware as
I start to answer it that I'm listening to music. Jazz. Chamber
ensemble jazz. Like a string quartet. You dig. Like maybe the
M.J.Q. Phone rings but I don't want to miss the music. I
hesitate. Or maybe I already have the phone at my ear. I'm
unhappy because I'm about to miss the concert, but, you know,
once I answered or decided to answer I wasn't hearing the
music anyway, so shit. I say hello. Hello who is it? Kind of in
a hurry. Annoyed you know because I've been interrupted.
Then you come on.

Buck. Buck, is that you?

She's gone, man.

Buck your magic twanger.

Then I look at the stage. The musicians are in tuxedos.
You know. Like penguins. And the darkness is not behind
them. Darkness is this crisp sharp hard kind of foreground
and the stage is behind it. I think maybe a steel curtain is
pulled in front of the four players, four of them, a quartet. I
think that's what's strange, different about the way the four
of them look. They are marooned far away behind this dark-

ness. The black curtain has been scissored precisely to sur-
round each silhouette, then seamlessly each player's been sewn
into the fabric. But a curtain wouldn't hang that way. A curtain has drapes and folds, people need room to move and
breathe so what I saw was crazy. Something inside of me says
no. I can't be seeing what I'm seeing, what I think I see. My
eyes readjust. Do a double take, you know. Figure-ground
reversal. Fish become birds, or birds fish. Except once you
make up your mind which it is, ain't no going back. You say,
Show me something else, this doesn't make sense. Then you're
stuck with what you got. The paper-thin men and thin paper
cut-out black screen come together in another way so I can
deal with what was up there on the stage.

It happened much quicker than I can tell it. I never
heard words, myself talking to myself. Just that blink. That
click. Before I can say, Hey, wait a minute. This ain't right.
Click. It's back to normal. I'm holding the phone. It's you.
The players are three-dimensional again. Onstage. Not pro-
jected on a screen. Not millions of white specks and black
specks floating, dancing. Their suits are not the curtain. Faces
not holes punched in the snow. The stage is not wearing them
anymore. I'm getting all that mess resolved in my mind. La-
di-da. But it's costing me. I can't go back. Dizzy almost. My
heart's thumping. I worry about everybody in the family's
high blood pressure. And there's still you on the phone.

Buck. Are you there? Zat you?

I'm scared to pick up the receiver. I've already been
through the conversation and I don't want to hear bad news
again. The phone rings and rings but I don't hear a thing. I
can't hang up. Because I haven't picked up yet. The piece
playing I know the title of because the xylophone man just
said it. Or part of the title. Europe's in it. Milan. Streets of

Milano. Or Milano Afternoon. I heard it announced. Before. When I was paying attention. Before you rang. Before I started getting sick inside my self and looking for an exit.

Did you ever think of titles as premonitions? Threats. Destiny. Most come after I've written or told a story many times but occasionally the first words name everything else that follows. And stop me when I've said enough. A threat. A destination. I might as well say it all. A title can be like death. Like dying and being born at the same time.

The audience begins to file out. Some people stand at their seats clapping but when it becomes clear the musicians aren't going to play anymore no matter how long or loud we applaud, the trick of slapping one hand against the other, like hundreds of trained seals, starts to feel, first to one, then another and finally to the entire group like a silly way to behave. One hand continues clapping in the void but all the rest split, leaving me stuck with the phone in mine, unplayed and exhausted passages of concert in my brain, a fear, a withering godawful fright that something terrible has happened or was going to happen.

Ping. Ping. The Chinese water torture drop of the phone no one is left to answer but me in the bright hall.

On the other hand some tunes need no introduction.

PRESENTS

I *stood on the bank ...*

Oh yes, she said. Oh yes and I did not know what she was yessing any more than I know how her voice, her yes reaches from wherever she is to wherever I am now, except it's like the ships seen from the bank of Jordan in that song sailing on, sailing on from there to here quietly as dream.

Big Mama. Big Mama. Doubling her not because she is not real enough once but because her life takes up so much space. I stare at her afraid to look away. Scared she'll be gone if I do. Scared I'll be gone.

Baby, you listen to your Big Mama now. Listen cause I ain't got nothing but mouth and time and hardly none that left.

He is saucer-eyed. Awkward. A big, nappy head.

She pats each nap and each awakes. A multitude stirring as she passes her old hand once in the air over the crown of his skull.

Love Jesus and love yourself and love those who love you, sugar. Those who don't love you don't love theyselves and shame on them. Nobody but Jesus can save their sorry souls.

She purses her lips. Her tongue pushes that hard-as-the-world bitter lemon into one cheek. She sucks on it. All the sour of it smears her old lips. She is Big Mama. No bones in her body. Even now, even this Christmas so close to death the bones cannot claim her. Nothing will crack or snap or buckle in her. In her lap he will curl and sleep and always find soft room to snuggle deeper. To fall. To sleep.

He remembers being big enough to crawl alone under her bed and little enough, little sweet doodlebug, you come on over here gimme some sugar, to sit upright and his head just grazes the beehive network of springs. Hiding under her bed and playing with the dust and light he raises and the tasseled knots of fringed chenille bedspread. Bed so high so you had to *climb* up on it. Mind you don't roll off, boy. He did not think *throne* but he knew her bed was raised high to be a special place, to be his Big Mama's bed.

So when she kneels beside the bed he hears the sigh of the room rushing together again over her head, sigh as the fist of her heart, the apron pocket of her chest empties and fills, the grunt and wheeze of his Big Mama dropping to one knee and lifts the spread and her arm disappears as if she's fishing for him under there. Come out, you little doodlebug rascal. I know you hiding in there. Boogeyman get you you don't come from under there. Her arm sweeps and he can see her fingers under the edge of the bed, inside the cave, though he is outside now and it's like being two places at once, hiding and looking for his ownself, watching her old hand, the fingers hooked, beckoning. C'mon out, you monkey you, sweeping a half inch off the floor, precisely at the level of the unfailing, fringed spread hanging off the side of the bed.

What she drags forth this Christmas Eve afternoon as he watches her kneeling beside the bed is wrapped in a blanket. Not him this time, but something covered with a sheet and swaddled in a woolly blanket. Shapeless. Then Big Mama digs into folds and flaps, uncovers woman curves, the taut shaft. There are long strings and a hole in the center. Gently as she goes she cannot help accidents that trick stirrings from the instrument. A bowl of jelly quivering. Perhaps all it needs is the play of her breath as she bends over it, serious and quiet as a child undressing a doll. Or the air all by its ownself is enough to agitate the strings when Big Mama finally has it laid bare across her bed.

The story as he's preached it so many times since is simple. A seven-year-old boy makes his grandmother a song. He intends to sing it for her Christmas Day but Christmas Eve afternoon she calls him into her bedroom and kneels and pulls a guitar wrapped in rags and blankets from under her bed. He is mesmerized and happy. He hugs his Big Mama and can't help telling her about the love song he's made up for her Christmas present. She says you better sing it for me now, baby, and he does and she smiles the whole time he sings. Then she lays out the sad tale of his life as a man. He'll rise in the world, sing for kings and queens but his gift for music will also drag him down to the depths of hell. She tells it gently, he is only a boy, with her eyes fixed on the ceiling and they fill up with tears. Oh yes. Oh yes, yes. Yes, Jesus. The life he must lead a secret pouring out of her. Emptying her. Already she's paying for the good and evil in him. Yes. Yes. She's quiet then. Still. They sit together on the side of her high bed till it's dark outside the window. He can't see snow but smells it, hears how silently it falls. She asks him, Sing my song one more time. His little Christmas gift song because he loves to sing and make rhymes and loves his Big Mama and the grace of sweet Jesus is heavy in this season of his birth. By the next morning his Big Mama is dead. The others come for Christmas Day, discover her. He's been awake since dawn, learning to pick out her song quietly on his new guitar. His mother and the rest of them bust in, stomp their snowy shoes in the hallway and Merry Christmas and where's Big Mama? They find her dead in bed and he's been playing ever since. Everything she prophesied right on the money, honey. To this very day. He's been up and he's been down and that's the way she told him it would be all the days of his life. Amen.

Each time in the middle of the story he thinks he won't ever need to tell it again. Scooted up under the skirt of Big Mama's bed. His mother comes over to visit and she fusses at him. You're too big a boy to be hiding go seek under Mama's bed. Don't let him play under there, Mama. Don't baby him. Time he start growing up.

His mother visits and takes a bath in Big Mama's iron tub. He sees her bare feet and bare ankles, her bare butt as he holds his breath and quiet as a spider slides to the edge and peeks up through the fringy spread. He lifts the covering to see better. Inch by inch. Quiet as snow. She has a big, round behind with hairs at the bottom. He thinks of water-melons and can't eat that fruit without guilt ever after. He watches her as she stands in front of the mirror of his grand-mother's chiffonier. His heart beats fast as it can. He's afraid she'll hear it, afraid she'll turn quickly and find his eye peeking up from under the covers at her. But when she does turn, it's slowly, slowly so he hears the rub of her bare heel on the

linoleum where the rug doesn't stretch to where she's standing. He drops the window of his hiding place. He's spared a
vision of the front of her. Titties. Pussycat between her legs.
Just ankles and bare feet till she's finished and wrapped
in one Big Mama's housecoats and asking for him in the
other room.

You been in here all this time? You been hiding under
there while I was dressing? Why didn't you say something, boy?

The story has more skins than an onion. And like an
onion it can cause a grown man to cry when he starts to
peeling it.

Or else it can go quick. Big Mama said, That's the most
beautiful song in the world. Thank you, precious. Thank you
and thank Jesus for bringing such a sweet boy to this old
woman.

Will you teach me how to play?

Your old grandmama don't know nothing bout such
things. She's tired besides. You learn your ownself. Just beat
on it like a drum till something come out sound good to you.

The music's in the box like the sword in the stone. Beat
it. Pound it. Chisel away. Then one day it gon sound good.
Gon slide loose easy as it slided in. Then it's smooth as but-
ter. Then it sings God's praise. Oh yes. Oh yes.

She gave him the guitar in Jesus' name. Amened it.
Prayed over it with him that Christmas Eve afternoon how
many years ago. Well, let's see. I was seven then and I'm an
old man now so that's how long it's been, that's how many
times I've preached the story.

My grandmother believed in raising a joyful noise unto
the Lord. Tambourines and foot stomping and gut-bucket piano rolls and drums and shouts and yes if you could find one

a mean guitar rocking like the ark in heavy seas till it gets good to everybody past the point of foot patting and finger popping in your chair past that till the whole congregation out they seats dancing in the air.

Something born that day and something died. His fate cooked up for him like a mess of black-eyed peas and ham hocks and he's been eating at the table of it ever since. Lean days and fat days.

Where did she find a guitar? Who'd played the instrument before it was his? Could it ever be his if other fingers had plucked the strings, run up and down the long neck? Grease and sweat ground into its wood, its metal strings. When he was at last alone with the gift she'd given him and told him not to play till Christmas, he'd peered into the hole in its belly. Held it by its fat hips and shook it to hear if anybody'd left money in there. If the right sound won't come out plucking it, there was always the meaty palm of his hand to knock sense in it.

How long did he hide in the church before he carried his box out on the street corner? How long for the Lord, how many licks for the Devil? How long before you couldn't tell one from the other? Him the last to know. Always.

A boy wonder. An evil hot blood Buddy Bolden Willie the Lion Robert Johnson wild man boy playing the fool and playing the cowboy fool shit out that thang, man. Yes. Oh yes.

And one day Praise God I said, Huh uh. No more. Thank you Jesus and broke it over my knee and cried cause I'd lost my Big Mama.

Atlantic City. Niggers pulling rickshaws up and down the Boardwalk. Naw. If I'm lying, I'm flying. They did, boy. Yes they did. Drugging white folks around behind them in these big carts. Like in China, man. Or wherever they keep them things. Saw that shit on the Boardwalk in Atlantic City, U.S. of A. Yeah. And niggers happy to be doing it. Collecting fabulous tips, they say. Hauling peckerwoods around. Not me. See, I knew better. I'd seen the world. Had me a gig in one those little splib clubs on Arctic Avenue. Enough to keep me in whiskey. Didn't need no pad. It was summer. Sleep on the beach. Or sleep with one the ladies dig my playing. A real bed, a shower every few days to scald the sand out my asshole. Living the life, partner. Till I woke up one morning in the gutter. Stone gutter, man. Like a dead rat. Head busted. Vomit all on my clothes. In broad daylight I'm lolling in the gutter, man. Said, Huh uh. No indeed. These the bonds of hell. Done fell clean off the ladder and I'm down in the pit. The goddamn gutter floor of the pit's bottom. I'm lost. Don't a living soul give one dime fuck about me and I don't neither.

That's when I hollered, Get me up from here, Big Mama. You said I'd rise and I did. You prophesied I'd fall and here I am. Now reach down and help me up. Gimme your soft silk purse old woman's hand and lift this crusty burden off the street. Take me back to your bosom. Rise and fall, you said. Well, I can't fall no further so carry me on up again. Please. Please. Big Mama. Reach down off the high side of your bed and bring me back.

Her fingers hooked like a eagle's beak. Holding a cloak of feathers fashioned from wings of fallen angels. Where you find this, Big Mama? How'm I spozed to play this thing? Beat it, you say. Pound it like a drum. Just step out in the air with it round your shoulders. Let the air take you and fly you on home. Squeeze it till it sound like you need it to sound. Good. Giant steps ain't nothing if they ain't falling up and falling down and carrying you far from this place to another.

Sailing. To meet me in the morning. On Jordan one day. Singing, Yes. Oh yes.

I stood on the bank ...

And my neck ached like I'd been lynched. Like I'd been laid out for dead and hard rock was my pillow and cold ground my bed.

Hard rock my pillow and help me today, Lord. Help me tell it. I scrambled to my feet and shook the sooty graveclothes and sand and scales and dust and feathers and morning blood off my shoulders. Skinny as a scarecrow. Funky as toejam. My mouth dry and my eyes scored by rusty razors, my tongue like a turtle forgot how to poke his head out his shell. Scrambled to my aching feet and there it was spread out over me the city of my dreams, Philadelphia all misbegotten and burnt crisp and sour sour at the roots as all my bad teefs.

Play it, son.

Bucka do. Bucka do little dee.

Black as sugar burnt to the bottom of a pan. And Big Mama told me. She said, Squeeze it to the last drop.

A simple story. Easy to tell to a stranger at the bar who will buy you a drink. Young boy and old woman. Christmastime. Reading each other's minds. Exchanging gifts of song. His fortune told. The brief, bright time of his music. How far it took him, how quickly gone. The candle flaring up, guttering, gone. He'd told it many times. Risen. Fallen. Up. Down. Rubs his crusty eyes and peers into a honey-colored room with no walls, feet scurry past his head, busy going every which way, sandals and brogans and sneakers and shiny Stacy-Adamses and pitter-pat of high-stepper high heels on the pavement as he lifts his head and goes over the whole business again, trying to settle once and for all who he must be and why it always ends this way his head on the hard rock of curbstone, the ships sailing on, sailing on.

The river is brass or blood or mud depending on the day, the season, the hour. Big Mama is where she is. He is here. Her voice plain as day in his ear. He wishes someone would pat him on his head and say everything's gon be all right.

THE TAMBOURINE LADY

Now *I lay me down to sleep* . . . there will be new shoes in the morning. New shoes and an old dress white as new. Starched white and stiff with petticoats whispering like angel wings and hair perfect as heat and grease can press it. There will be hands to shake as she rises from the curb onto the one broad step that took you off Homewood Avenue, which was nowhere, to the red doors of the church that were wide enough to let the whole world in but narrow too, narrower than your narrow hips, child, eye of the needle straight and narrow, don't make no mistake. Hands to help her across the threshold, through the tall red doors, from hard pavement that burned in summer, froze in winter, to the deep cushion of God's crimson carpet. She's unsteady as she passes to His world. Like that first step from moving stairs downtown in Kaufmann's Department Store when you always think you're falling, pitched down and about to be cracked to pieces on the shiny checkerboard floor rushing up to mire your feet. At the church door her mother's hand, the gloved hand of Miss Payton to help her through. Miss Payton all in white, white veil, white gloves, white box tied over her hair with a silky white bandage. Breath might catch in her throat, her heart stutter but she wouldn't fall. She'd catch hold to old Miss Payton's hand, soft and white as a baby rabbit. Miss Payton smelling like Johnson's baby powder, who'd say, Bless you, sweet darling daughter, so the step up did not trip you, the wide doors slam in your face.

New shoes pinched your feet. Too big, too small, too much money, too ugly for anybody to be caught dead in. The white ladies who sold them would stick any old thing on your feet and smile at your mama and say, Just right. But sometimes when her feet in new shoes she'd forget how they felt, and she'd float. Couldn't take her eyes off them, stepping where she stepped, she follows them everywhere they go, click-clack cleats on the bottoms to save the heels and soles. They are new and shiny and for a while she's brand-new and shiny in them. Now she's nobody, nowhere, kneeled down beside her bed, remembering into the silence of God's ear a little girl in new shoes that didn't belong to her, that wouldn't fit. Her toes are drawn up curly, black against pink underskin. She dreams white anklets with a lacy band around the top. Dreams meat on her bones so socks don't slip down to her shoe tops.

If you polished old shoes, you could see your face inside. New ones come with your face in them. In the morning she'd take them out the box polish them anyway and then wash and dry her face and clean her hands and tug the purple Buds of Promise sash straight. Make sure of everything in the mirror.

On the threshold of the African Methodist Episcopal Zion Church there will be a mirror in the gray sky, a mirror in the brick walls, a mirror in her mother's eyes and in the hand of Miss Payton reaching for hers, patting her ashy skin, promising she will not fall.

She closes her eyes and hears tambourines. Crashing like a pocketful of silver in her daddy's pants when he stuck in his hand and rummaged round, teasing out a piece of change for her. Like somebody saying dish dish dish dish and every dish piled high with something good to eat.

Dish. Dish.

And if I die ... before I wake. You walk funny because more crack than sidewalk some places on the way home from school. You sneak out into Hamilton Avenue to get past the real bad busted-up part where sidewalk's in little pieces like a broken jar.

You looked both ways up and down Hamilton Avenue but you know you might die. *A thousand times. I've told you a thousand times to stay out of Hamilton Avenue, girl.* But if the sidewalk looked like a witch's face you'd rather get runned over than step on a crack and break your mama's back. So you looked both ways up and down the street like Mama always said. You looked and listened and hoped you wouldn't get hit like little fat Angela everybody called Jelly who was playing in Cassina Way and the car mashed her up against the fence where you can still see the spot to this day.

She feels mashed like Jelly when Tommy Bonds pushes her down. He laughs and calls her crybaby. Says, You ain't hurt and runs away. But she ain't no crybaby over no little blood snot on her knee. She cries cause he hurt her mama. Pushed her into the spider web of cracks cause he knew what she was playing. She'd told him her secret because she thought they were friends. But he never really was. He hates her and pushes her right dead down in a whole mess of snakes. She cries cause she's trapped, can't get out without stepping on more. Every crack a bone in her mama's back. He hates her. He follows her after school and calls her nasty stuck-up bitch till she stops, hands on hips, and hollers, Boy, I ain't studying you. You ain't nothing, Tommy Bonds, and wiggles her butt at him, then she is running, tearing down the sidewalk, scared and happy to have him after her again no matter what he wants to do. She would forgive him. Forgive his bad words, forgive his lies, forgive him for telling her secrets to everybody. She is forgiving, forgetting everything as he flies down Hamilton after her. She knows he can't catch her if she doesn't want to be caught. Says to herself, See what he wants now. Stops, hands on hips, at the edge of the worst busted-up place. *Girl, don't you dare set foot in that traffic on Hamilton Avenue.* And all he wants is to shove her down. Kill her mama.

She'd told Tommy Bonds her secret. He'd sneaked out into the street with her. Played her game and the cars whipping past on Hamilton Avenue had never been louder, closer, their wind up under her clothes as they ran the twenty steps past Wicked Witch Face City. And never had she cared less about getting mashed because who ever heard of a car killing two at a time.

Tommy, Tommy, Tommy *Bonds.* If she didn't duck just in time the rope would cut off her neck. If she didn't bounce high enough there go her cut-off feet hopping down the street all by they ownselves. Say it, girl. Say it. *Bonds* was when the rope popped the ground. *Tommy* three fast times while the loop turned lazy in the air.

Shake it to the east, Shake it to the west. Now tell the one you love the best. Say it loud and proud, girl. We ain't turning for nothing.

Tommy-Tommy-Tommy *Bonds.*

She is not crying because it hurts. A little snotty-looking blood. Scab on her knee next day. That's all. That's not why I'm crying, Mister Smarty-pants. Mister Know-it-all. But she can't say his name, can't say what she's thinking because the tears in her nose and ears and mouth might come crashing down and she'd be a puddle. Nasty brown puddle in the middle of the street.

Pray the Lord my soul to take.

The lady who beat the tambourine and sang in church was a Russell. Tomorrow was church so she'd see the Russells, the Strothers, Bells, Frenches, Pattersons, Whites, Bonds. Tomorrow was church so this was Saturday night and her mama ironing white things in the kitchen and her daddy away so long he mize well be dead and the new patent-leather shoes in their box beneath her side of the bed be worn out before he sees them. She thinks about how long it takes to get to the end of your prayers, how the world might be over and gone while you still saying the words to yourself. Words her mama taught her, words her mama said her mother had taught her so somebody would always be saying them world without end amen. So God would not forget His children. Saying the words this Saturday night, saying them tomorrow morning so He would not forget. Tommy Tommy Tommy Bonds. Words like doors. You open one wide and peek inside and everybody in there, strolling up and down the red aisles, singing, shaking hands. People she wanted to see and people she didn't know and the ones she'd been seeing all her life. People she hates.

God bless ... Words like the rope right on time slapping the pavement, snapping her heart. Her feet in new shoes she knows better than to be wearing outside playing in the street girl and they break and she falls and falls and if she had one wish it would be let me hear the lady sing her tambourine song tomorrow morning in church.

LITTLE BROTHER

For Judy

Penny, don't laugh. Come on now, you know I love that little critter. And anyway, how you so sure it didn't work?

Tylenol?

Yep. Children's liquid Tylenol. The children's formula's not as strong and he was only a pup. Poured two teaspoons in his water dish. I swear it seemed to help.

Children's Tylenol.

With the baby face on it. You know. Lapped it up like he understood it was good for him. He's alive today, ain't he? His eye cleared up, too.

You never told me this story before.

Figured you'd think I was crazy.

His eye's torn up again.

You know Little Brother got to have his love life. Out tomcatting around again. Sticking his nose in where it don't belong. Bout once a month he disappears from here. Used to worry. Now I know he'll be slinking back in three or four days with his tail dragging. Limping around spraddle-legged. Sleeping all day cause his poor dickie's plumb wore out.

Geral.

It's true. Little Brother got it figured better than most people. Do it till you can't do it no more. Come home half dead and then you can mind your own business for a while.

Who you voting for?

None of them fools. Stopped paying them any mind long time ago.

I hear what you're saying, but this is special. It's for president.

One I would have voted for. One I would have danced for buck naked up on Homewood Avenue, is gone. My pretty preacher man's gone. Shame the way they pushed him right off the stage. The rest them all the same. Once they in they all dirty dogs. President's the one cut the program before I could get my weather stripping. Every time the kitchen window rattles and I see my heat money seeping out the cracks, I curse that mean old Howdy Doody turkey-neck clown.

How's Ernie?

Mr. White's fine.

Mama always called him Mr. White. And Ote said *Mr. White* till we shamed him out of it.

I called Ernie that too before we were married. When he needed teasing. Formal like Mama did. *Mr. White.* He was *Mr. White* to her till the day she died.

But Mama loved him.

Of course she did. Once she realized he wasn't trying to steal me away. Thing is she never had that to worry about. Not in a million years. I'd have never left Mama. Even when Ote was alive and staying here. She's been gone all these years but first thing I think every morning when I open my eyes is,

You OK, Mama? I'm right here, Mama. Be there in a minute, to get you up. I still wake up hoping she's all right. That she didn't need me during the night. That I'll be able to help her through the day.

Sometimes I don't know how you did it.

Gwan, girl. If things had been different, if you didn't have a family of your own, if I'd had the children, you would have been the one to stay here and take care of Mama.

I guess you're right. Yes. I would.

No way one of us wouldn't have taken care of her. You. Ote. Sis or me. Made sense for me and Ote to do it. We stayed home. If you hadn't married, you'd have done it. And not begrudged her one moment of your time.

Ote would have been sixty in October.

I miss him. It's just Ernie and me and the dogs rattling around in this big house now. Some things I have on my mind I never get to say to anybody because I'm waiting to tell them to Ote.

He was a good man. I can still see Daddy pulling him around in that little wagon. The summer Ote had rheumatic fever and the doctor said he had to stay in bed and Daddy made him that wagon and propped him up with pillows and pulled him all over the neighborhood. Ote bumping along up and down Cassina Way with his thumb in his mouth half sleep and Daddy just as proud as a peacock. After three girls, finally had him a son to show off.

Ote just about ran me away from here when I said I was keeping Little Brother. Two dogs are enough, Geraldine. Why would you bring something looking like that in the house? Let that miserable creature go on off and find a decent place to die. You know how Ote could draw hisself up like John French. Let you know he was half a foot taller than you and carrying all that John French weight. Talked like him, too. *Geraldine*, looking down on me saying all the syllables of my name like Daddy used to when he was mad at me. *Geraldine*. Run that miserable thing away from here. When it sneaks up under the porch and dies, you won't be the one who has to get down on your hands and knees and crawl under there to drag it out.

But he was the one wallpapered Little Brother's box with insulation, wasn't he? The one who hung a flap of rug over the door to keep out the wind.

The one who cried like a baby when Pup-pup was hit.

Didn't he see it happen?

Almost. He was turning the corner of Finance. Heard the brakes screech. The bump. He was so mad. Carried Pup-pup and laid him on the porch. Fussing the whole time at Pup-pup. You stupid dog. You stupid dog. How many times have I told you not to run in the street. Like Pup-pup could hear him. Like Pup-pup could understand him if he'd been alive. Ote stomped in the house and up the stairs. Must have washed his hands fifteen minutes. Running water like we used to do when Mama said we better not get out of bed once we were in the bed so running and running that water till it made us pee one long last time before we went to sleep.

What are you girls doing up there wasting all that water? I'ma be up there in ten minutes and you best be under the covers.

Don't be the last one. Don't be on the toilet and just starting to pee good and bumpty-bump here she comes up the steps and means what she says. Uh ohh. It's Niagara Falls and you halfway over and ain't no stopping now. So you just sit there squeezing your knees together and work on that smile you don't hardly believe and she ain't buying one bit when she brams open the door and Why you sitting there grinning like a Chessy cat, girl. I thought I told youall ten minutes ago to get in bed.

Ote washed and washed and washed. I didn't see much blood. Pup-pup looked like Pup-pup laid out there on the porch. Skinny as he was you could always see his ribs moving when he slept. So it wasn't exactly Pup-pup because it was too still. But it wasn't torn up bloody or runned-over looking either.

Whatever Ote needed to wash off, he took his time. He was in the bathroom fifteen minutes, then he turned off the faucets and stepped over into his room and shut the door but you know how the walls and doors in this house don't stop nothing so I could hear him crying when I went out in the hall to call up and ask him if he was all right, ask him what he wanted to do with Pup-pup. I didn't say a word. Just stood there thinking about lots of things. The man crying on his bed was my baby brother. And I'd lived with him all my life in the same house. Now it was just the two of us. Me in the hall listening. Him on his bed, a grown man sobbing cause he's too mad to do anything else. You and Sis moved out first. Then Daddy gone. Then Mama. Just two of us left and two mutts in the house I've lived in all my life. Then it would be one of us left. Then the house empty. I thought some such sorrowful thoughts. And thought of poor Pup-pup. And that's when I decided to say yes to Ernie White after all those years of no.

Dan. If you want a slice of this sweet potato pie you better come in here now and get it. It's leaving here fast. They're carting it away like sweet potato pie's going out of style.

It's his favorite.

That's why I bake one every time old Danny boy's home from school.

Did he tell you he saw Marky at Mellon Park?

No.

Dan was playing ball and Marky was in a bunch that hangs around on the sidelines. He said Marky recognized him. Mumbled hi. Not much more than that. He said Marky didn't look good. Not really with the others but sitting off to the side, on the ground, leaning back against the fence. Dan went over to him and Marky nodded or said hi, enough to let Danny know it really was Marky and not just somebody who looked like Marky, or Marky's ghost because Dan said it wasn't the Marky he remembered. It's the Marky who's been driving us all crazy.

At least he's off Homewood Avenue.

That's good I suppose.

Good and bad. Like everything else. He can move hisself off the Avenue and I'm grateful for that but it also means he can go and get hisself in worse trouble. A healthy young man with a good head on his shoulders and look at him. It's pitiful. Him and lots the other young men like zombies nodding on Homewood Avenue. Pitiful. But as long as he stays on Homewood the cops won't hassle him. What if he goes off and tries to rob somebody or break in somebody's house? Marky has no idea half the time who he is or what he's doing. He's like a baby. He couldn't get away with anything. Just hurt hisself or hurt somebody trying.

What can we do?

We kept him here as long as we could. Ernie talked and talked to him. Got him a job when he dropped out of school. Talked and talked and did everything he could. Marky just let hisself go. He stopped washing. Wore the same clothes night and day. And he was always such a neat kid. A dresser. Stood in front of the mirror for days arranging himself just so for the ladies. I don't understand it. He just fell apart, Penny. You've seen him. You remember how he once was. How many times have I called you and cried over the phone about Marky? Only so much any of us could do, then Ernie said it was too dangerous to have him in the house. Wouldn't leave me here alone with Marky. I about went out my mind then. Not safe in my own house with this child I'd taken in and raised. My husband's nephew who'd been like my own child, who I'd watched grow into a man. Not safe. Nothing to do but let him roam the streets.

None of the agencies or programs would help. What else could you do, Geral?

They said they couldn't take him till he did something wrong. What kind of sense does that make? They'll take him after the damage is done. After he freezes to death sleeping on a bench up in Homewood Park. Or's killed by the cops. Or stark raving foaming at the mouth. They'll take him then. Sorry, Mrs. White, our hands are tied.

Sorry, Mrs. White. Just like the receptionist at Dr. Franklin's. That skinny, pinched-nosed *sorry, Mrs. Whatever-your-name-is* cause they don't give a good goddamn they just doing their job and don't hardly want to be bothered, especially if it's you, and you're black and poor and can't do nothing for them but stand in line and wait your turn and as far as they're concerned you can wait forever.

Did I tell you what happened to me in Dr. Franklin's office, Penny? Five or six people in the waiting room. All of them white. Chattering about this and that. They don't know me and I sure don't know none of them but cause they see my hair ain't kinky and my skin's white as theirs they get on colored people and then it's niggers after they warm up awhile. Ain't niggers enough to make you throw up? Want everything and not willing to work a lick. Up in your face now like they think they own the world. Pushing past you in line at the A&P. Got so now you can't ride a bus without taking your life in your hands. This city's not what it used to be. Used to be a decent place to live till they started having all those nigger babies and now a white person's supposed to grin and bear it. It's three women talking mostly and the chief witch's fat and old as I am. And listen to this. She's afraid of being raped. She hears about white women attacked every day and she's fed up. Then she says, It's time somebody did something, don't you think? Killing's too good for those animals. Looking over at me with her head cocked and her little bit of nappy orange hair got the nerve to google at me like she's waiting for me to wag my head and cluck like the rest of those hens. Well I didn't say a word but the look I gave that heifer froze her mouth shut and kept it shut. Nobody uttered a word for the half hour till it was my turn to see Dr. Franklin. Like when we were bad and Mama'd sit us down and dare us to breathe till she said we could. They're lucky that's all I did. Who she think want to rape her? What self-respecting man, black, white, green or polka dot gon take his life in his hands scuffling with that mountain of blubber?

Geral.

Don't laugh. It wasn't funny. Rolling her Kewpie-doll eyes at me. Ain't niggers terrible? I was about to terrible her ass if I heard *nigger* one more time in her mouth.

Listen at you. Leave that poor woman alone. How old's Little Brother now?

We've had him nine years. A little older than that. Just

a wee thing when he arrived on the porch. *Geraldine.* You
don't intend bringing that scrawny rat into the house, do you?

And the funny thing is Little Brother must have heard
Ote and been insulted. Cause Little Brother never set foot
inside the front door. Not in the whole time he's lived here.
Not a paw. First he just made a bed in the rags I set out by
the front door. Then the cardboard box on the front porch.
Then when he grew too big for that Ote built his apartment
under the porch. I just sat and rocked the whole time Ote
hammering and sawing and cussing when the boards wouldn't
stay straight or wouldn't fit the way he wanted them too.
Using Daddy's old rusty tools. Busy as a beaver all day long
and I'm smiling to myself but I didn't say a mumbling word,
girl. If I had let out so much as one signifying I-told-you-so
peep, Ote woulda built another box and nailed me up inside.
Little Brother went from rags to his own private apartment
and in that entire time he's never been inside the house once.
I coaxed him, Here, puppy, here, puppy, puppy, and put
his food inside the hallway but that's one stubborn creature.
Little Brother'd starve to death before he'd walk through the
front door.

He about drove Pup-pup crazy. Pup-pup would sneak out
and eat Little Brother's food. Drag his rags away and hide
them. Snap and growl but Little Brother paid him no mind.
Pup-pup thought Little Brother was nuts. Living outdoors in
the cold. Not fighting back. Carrying a teddy bear around in
his mouth. Peeing in his own food so Pup-pup wouldn't bother
it. Pup-pup was so jealous. Went to his grave still believing
he had to protect his territory. Pup-pup loved to roam the
streets, but bless his heart, he became a regular stay-at-home.
Figured he better hang around and wait for Little Brother to

make his move. Sometimes I think that's why Pup forgot how to act in the street. In such a hurry to get out and get back, he got himself runned over.

That reminds me of Maria Indovina. Danny wanted me to walk around the neighborhood with him. He wanted to see the places we're always talking about. Mr. Conley's lot. Klein's store. Aunt Aida's. Hazel and Nettie's. Showed him the steps up to Nettie's and told him she never came down them for thirty years. He said, In youall's tales these sounded like the highest, steepest steps in creation. I said they were. Told him I'd follow you and Sis cause I was scared to go first. And no way in the world I'd be first coming back down. They didn't seem like much to him even when I reminded him we were just little girls and Aunt Hazel and Cousin Nettie like queens who lived in another world. Anyway, we were back behind Susquehanna where we used to play and there's a high fence back there on top of the stone wall. It's either a new fence or newly painted but the wall's the same old wall where the bread truck crushed poor Maria Indovina. I told him we played together in those days. Black kids and white kids. Mostly Italian then. Us and the Italians living on the same streets and families knowing each other by name. I told him and he said that's better than it is today. Tried to explain to him we lived on the same streets but didn't really mix. Kids playing together and Hello, how are you, Mr. So-and-so, Mrs. So-and-so, that and a little after-hours undercover mixing. Only time I ever heard Mama curse was when she called Tina Sabettelli a whorish bitch.

John French wasn't nobody's angel.

Well, I wasn't discussing none of that with Dan. I did tell him about the stain on the wall and how we were afraid to pass by it alone.

Speaking of white people how's your friend from up the street?

Oh, Vicki's fine. Her dresses are still too mini for my old fuddy-duddy taste. But no worse than what the other girls wearing. Her little girl Carolyn still comes by every afternoon for her piece of candy. She's a lovely child. My blue-eyed sweetheart. I worry about her. Auntie Gerry, I been a good girl today. You got me a sweet, Auntie Gerry? Yes, darling, I do. And I bring her whatever we have around the house. She'll stand in line with the twins from next door, and Becky and Rashad. They're my regulars but some the others liable to drop by, too. Hi, Aunt Gerry. Can I have a piece of candy, please? When they want something they're so nice and polite, best behaved lil devils in Homewood.

Yes, my friend Vicki's fine. Not easy being the only white person in the neighborhood. I told Fletcher and them to leave her alone. And told her she better respect herself a little more cause they sure won't if she don't. Those jitterbugs don't mean any harm, but boys will be boys. And she's not the smartest young lady in the world. These slicksters around here, you know how they are, hmmph. She better be careful is what I told her. She didn't like hearing what I said but I've noticed her carrying herself a little different when she walks by. Saw her dressed up real nice in Sears in East Liberty last week and she ducked me. I know why, but it still hurt me. Like it hurts me to think my little sugar Carolyn will be calling people niggers someday. If she don't already.

Did you love Ernie all those years you kept him waiting?

Love?

You know what I mean. Love.

Love love?

Love love love. You know what I'm asking you.

Penny. Did you love Billy?

Five children. Twenty-seven years off and on before he jumped up and left for good. I must have. Some of the time.

Real love? Hootchy-gootchy cooing and carrying on?

What did you say? Hootchy-koo? Is that what you said? To tell the truth I can't hardly remember. I must of had an operation when I was about eleven or twelve. Cut all that romance mess out. What's love got to do with anything, anyway.

You asked me first.

Wish I'd had the time. Can you picture Billy and Ernie dancing the huckle-buck, doing the hootchy-koo?

Whoa, girl. You gonna start me laughing.

Hootchy-gootchy-koo. Wish I'd had the time. Maybe it ain't too late. Here's a little hootchy-gootchy-koo for you.

Watch out. You're shaking the table. Whoa. Look at my drink.

Can't help it. I got the hootchy-goos. I'm in love.

Hand me one of those napkins.

Gootchy-gootchy-goo.

Behave now. The kids staring at us. Sitting here acting like two old fools.

So you think I ought to try Tylenol?

Two things for sure. Didn't kill Little Brother. And Princess is sick. Now the other sure thing is it might help Princess and it might not. Make sure it's the baby face. Kids' strength. Try that first.

I just might.

No you won't. You're still laughing at me.

No I'm not. I'm smiling thinking about Ote hammering

and sawing an apartment for Little Brother and you rocking on the porch trying to keep your mouth shut.

Like to bust, girl.

But you didn't.

Held it in to this very day. Till I told you.

Hey, youall. Leave a piece of sweet potato pie for your cousin, Dan. It's his favorite.

FEVER

To Matthew Carey, Esq., who fled Philadelphia
in its hour of need and upon his return published a libelous account of the behavior of black
nurses and undertakers, thereby injuring all people of my race and especially those without
whose unselfish, courageous labours the city
could not have survived the late calamity.

Consider Philadelphia from its centrical situa-
tion, the extent of its commerce, the number of
its artificers, manufacturers and other circum-
stances, to be to the United States what the heart
is to the human body in circulating the blood.

Robert Morris, 1777.

He stood staring through a tall window at the last days of
November. The trees were barren women starved for love and
they'd stripped off all their clothes, but nobody cared. And
not one of them gave a fuck about him, sifting among them,

weightless and naked, knowing just as well as they did, no hands would come to touch them, warm them, pick leaves off the frozen ground and stick them back in place. Before he'd gone to bed a flutter of insects had stirred in the dark outside his study. Motion worrying the corner of his eye till he turned and focused where light pooled on the deck, a cone in which he could trap slants of snow so they materialized into wet, gray feathers that blotted against the glass, the planks of the deck. If he stood seven hours, dark would come again. At some point his reflection would hang in the glass, a ship from the other side of the world, docked in the ether. Days were shorter now. A whole one spent wondering what goes wrong would fly away, fly in the blink of an eye.

Perhaps, *perhaps it may be acceptable to the reader to know how we found the sick affected by the sickness; our opportunities of hearing and seeing them have been very great. They were taken with a chill, a headache, a sick stomach, with pains in their limbs and back, this was the way the sickness in general began, but all were not affected alike, some appeared but slightly affected with some of these symptoms, what confirmed us in the opinion of a person being smitten was the colour of their eyes.*

Victims in this low-lying city perished every year, and some years were worse than others, but the worst by far was the long hot dry summer of '93, when the dead and dying wrested control of the city from the living. Most who were able, fled. The rich to their rural retreats, others to relatives and friends in the countryside or neighboring towns. Some simply left, with no fixed destination, the prospect of privation or starvation on the road preferable to cowering in their homes awaiting the fever's fatal scratching at their door. Busy streets deserted, commerce halted, members of families shunning one another, the sick abandoned to suffer and die alone. Fear ruled. From August when the first cases of fever appeared below Water Street, to November when merciful frosts ended the infestation, the city slowly deteriorated, as if it, too, could suffer the terrible progress of the disease: fever, enfeeblement, violent vomiting and diarrhea, helplessness, delirium, settled dejection when patients *concluded they must go (so the phrase for dying was), and therefore in a kind of fixed determined state of mind went off.*

In some it raged more furiously than in others—some have languished for seven and ten days, and appeared to get better the day, or some hours before they died, while others were cut off in one, two or three days, but their complaints were similar. Some lost their reason and raged with all the fury madness could produce, and died in strong convulsions. Others retained their reason to the last, and seemed rather to fall asleep than die.

Yellow fever: an acute infectious disease of subtropical and tropical New World areas, caused by a filterable virus transmitted by a mosquito of the genus *Aëdes* and characterized by jaundice and dark colored vomit resulting from hemorrhages. Also called *yellow jack.*

Dengue: an infectious, virulent tropical and subtropical disease transmitted by mosquitos and characterized by fever, rash and severe pains in the joints. Also called *breakbone fever, dandy.* [Spanish, of African origin, akin to Swahili *kindinga.*]

Curled in the black hold of the ship he wonders why his life on solid green earth had to end, why the gods had chosen this new habitation for him, floating, chained to other captives, no air, no light, the wooden walls shuddering, battered, as if some madman is determined to destroy even this last pitiful refuge where he skids in foul puddles of waste, bumping other bodies, skinning himself on splintery beams and planks, always moving, shaken and spilled like palm nuts in the diviner's fist, and Esu casts his fate, constant motion, tethered to an iron ring.

In the darkness he can't see her, barely feels her light touch on his fevered skin. Sweat thick as oil but she doesn't mind, straddles him, settles down to do her work. She enters him and draws his blood up into her belly. When she's full, she pauses, dreamy, heavy. He could kill her then; she wouldn't care. But he doesn't. Listens to the whine of her wings lifting till the whimper is lost in the roar and crash of waves, creaking wood, prisoners groaning. If she returns tomorrow and carries away another drop of him, and the next day and the next, a drop each day, enough days, he'll be gone. Shrink to nothing, slip out of this iron noose and disappear.

Aëdes aegypti: a mosquito of the family *Culicidae*, genus *Aëdes* in which the female is distinguished by a long proboscis for sucking blood. This winged insect is a vector (an organism that carries pathogens from one host to another) of yellow

fever and dengue. [New Latin *Aëdes*, from Greek *aedes*, un-
pleasant: *a* −, not + *edos*, pleasant . . .]

All things arrive in the waters and waters carry all things away.
So there is no beginning or end, only the waters' flow, ebb,
flood, trickle, tides emptying and returning, salt seas and riv-
ers and rain and mist and blood, the sun drowning in an ocean
of night, wet sheen of dawn washing darkness from our eyes.
This city is held in the water's palm. A captive as surely as I
am captive. Long fingers of river, Schuylkill, Delaware, the
rest of the hand invisible; underground streams and channels
feed the soggy flesh of marsh, clay pit, sink, gutter, stagnant
pool. What's not seen is heard in the suck of footsteps through
spring mud of unpaved streets. Noxious vapors that sting your
eyes, cause you to gag, spit and wince are evidence of a presence, the dead hand cupping this city, the poisons that cir-
culate through it, the sweat on its rotting flesh.

No one has asked my opinion. No one will. Yet I have
seen this fever before, and though I can prescribe no cure, I
could tell stories of other visitations, how it came and stayed
and left us, the progress of disaster, its several stages, its
horrors and mitigations. My words would not save one life,
but those mortally affrighted by the fever, by the prospect of
universal doom, might find solace in knowing there are limits
to the power of this scourge that has befallen us, that some,
yea, most will survive, that this condition is temporary, a
season, that the fever must disappear with the first deep
frosts and its disappearance is as certain as the fact it will
come again.

They say the rat's-nest ships from Santo Domingo
brought the fever. Frenchmen and their black slaves fleeing

black insurrection. Those who've seen Barbados's distemper say our fever is its twin born in the tropical climate of the hellish Indies. I know better. I hear the drum, the forest's heartbeat, pulse of the sea that chains the moon's wandering, the spirit's journey. Its throb is source and promise of all things being connected, a mirror storing everything, forgetting nothing. To explain the fever we need no boatloads of refugees, ragged and wracked with killing fevers, bringing death to our shores. We have bred the affliction within our breasts. Each solitary heart contains all the world's tribes, and its precarious dance echoes the drum's thunder. We are our ancestors and our children, neighbors and strangers to ourselves. Fever descends when the waters that connect us are clogged with filth. When our seas are garbage. The waters cannot come and go when we are shut off one from the other, each in his frock coat, wig, bonnet, apron, shop, shoes, skin, behind locks, doors, sealed faces, our blood grows thick and sluggish. Our bodies void infected fluids. Then we are dry and cracked as a desert country, vital parts wither, all dust and dry bones inside. Fever is a drought consuming us from within. Discolored skin caves in upon itself, we burn, expire.

I regret there is so little comfort in this explanation. It takes into account neither climatists nor contagionists, flies in the face of logic and reason, the good doctors of the College of Physicians who would bleed us, purge us, quarantine, plunge us in icy baths, starve us, feed us elixirs of bark and wine, sprinkle us with gunpowder, drown us in vinegar according to the dictates of their various healing sciences. Who, then, is this foolish, old man who receives his wisdom from pagan drums in pagan forests? Are these the delusions of one whose brain the fever has already begun to gnaw? Not quite. True, I have survived other visitations of the fever, but while it prowls this city, I'm in jeopardy again as you are, because I claim no immunity, no magic. The messenger who bears the news of my death will reach me precisely at the stroke determined when it was determined I should tumble from the void and taste air the first time. Nothing is an accident. Fever grows in the secret places of our hearts, planted there when one of us decided to sell one of us to another. The drum must pound ten thousand thousand years to drive that evil away.

Fires burn on street corners. Gunshots explode inside wooden houses. Behind him a carter's breath expelled in low, labored pants warns him to edge closer to housefronts forming one wall of a dark, narrow, twisting lane. Thick wheels furrow the unpaved street. In the fire glow the cart stirs a shimmer of dust, faint as a halo, a breath smear on a mirror. Had the man locked in the traces of the cart cursed him or was it just a wheeze of exertion, a complaint addressed to the unforgiving weight of his burden? Creaking wheels, groaning wood, plodding footsteps, the cough of dust, bulky silhouette blackened as it lurches into brightness at the block's end. All gone in a moment. Sounds, motion, sight extinguished. What remained, as if trapped by a lid clamped over the lane, was the stench of dead bodies. A stench cutting through the ubiquitous pall of vinegar and gunpowder. Two, three, four corpses being hauled to Potter's Field, trailed by the unmistakable wake of decaying flesh. He'd heard they raced their carts to the burial ground. Two or three entering Potter's Field from different directions would acknowledge one another with challenges, raised fists, gather their strength for a last dash to the open trenches where they tip their cargoes. Their brethren would wager, cheer, toast the victor with tots of rum. He could hear the rumble of coffins crashing into a common grave, see the comical chariots bouncing, the men's legs pumping, faces contorted by fires that blazed all night at the burial ground. Shouting and curses would hang in the torpid night air, one more nightmare troubling the city's sleep.

He knew this warren of streets as well as anyone. Night or day he could negotiate the twists and turnings, avoid cul-de-sacs, find the river even if his vision was obscured in tunnel-like alleys. He anticipated when to duck a jutting signpost, knew how to find doorways where he was welcome, wooden steps down to a cobbled terrace overlooking the water where his shod foot must never trespass. Once beyond the grand houses lining one end of Water Street, in this quarter of hovels, beneath these wooden sheds leaning shoulder to shoulder were cellars and caves dug into the earth, poorer men's dwellings under these houses of the poor, an invisible region where his people burrow, pull earth like blanket and quilt round themselves to shut out cold and dampness, sleeping multitudes to a room, stacked and crosshatched and spoon fashion, themselves the only fuel, heat of one body passed to others and passed back from all to one. Can he blame the lucky ones who are strong enough to pull the death carts, who celebrate and leap and roar all night around the bonfires? Why should they return here? Where living and dead, sick and well must lie face to face, shivering or sweltering on the same dank floor.

Below Water Street the alleys proliferate. Named and nameless. He knows where he's going but fever has transformed even the familiar. He'd been waiting in Dr. Rush's entrance hall. An English mirror, oval framed in scalloped brass, drew him. He watched himself glide closer, a shadow, a blur, then the shape of his face materialized from silken depths. A mask he did not recognize. He took the thing he

saw and murmured to it. Had he once been in control? Could
he tame it again? Like a garden ruined overnight, pillaged,
overgrown, trampled by marauding beasts. He stares at the
chaos until he can recall familiar contours of earth, seasons
of planting, harvesting, green shoots, nodding blossoms, scrap-
ing, digging, watering. Once upon a time he'd cultivated this
thing, this plot of flesh and blood and bone, but what had it
become? Who owned it now? He'd stepped away. His eyes
constructed another face and set it there, between him and
the wizened old man in the glass. He'd aged twenty years in
a glance and the fever possessed the same power to alter
suddenly what it touched. This city had grown ancient and
fallen into ruin in two months since early August, when the
first cases of fever appeared. Something in the bricks, mortar,
beams and stones had gone soft, had lost its permanence.
When he entered sickrooms, walls fluttered, floors buckled.
He could feel roofs pressing down. Putrid heat expanding. In
the bodies of victims. In rooms, buildings, streets, neighborhoods. Membranes that preserved the integrity of substances
and shapes, kept each in its proper place, were worn thin. He
could poke his finger through yellowed skin. A stone wall. The
eggshell of his skull. What should be separated was running
together. Threatened to burst. Nothing contained the way it
was supposed to be. No clear lines of demarcation. A mongrel
city. Traffic where there shouldn't be traffic. An awful void
opening around him, preparing itself to hold explosions of
bile, vomit, gushing bowels, ooze, sludge, seepage.

Earlier in the summer, on a July afternoon, he'd tried to
escape the heat by walking along the Delaware. The water was
unnaturally calm, isolated into stagnant pools by outcroppings
of wharf and jetty. A shelf of rotting matter paralleled the
river edge. As if someone had attempted to sweep what was

unclean and dead from the water. Bones, skins, entrails, torn carcasses, unrecognizable tatters and remnants broomed into a neat ridge. No sigh of the breeze he'd sought, yet fumes from the rim of garbage battered him in nauseating waves, a palpable medium intimate as wind. Beyond the tidal line of refuge, a pale margin lapped clean by receding waters. Then the iron river itself, flat, dark, speckled by sores of foam that puckered and swirled, worrying the stillness with a life of their own.

Spilled. Spoiled. Those words repeated themselves endlessly as he made his rounds. Dr. Rush had written out his portion, his day's share from the list of dead and dying. He'd purged, bled, comforted and buried victims of the fever. In and out of homes that had become tombs, prisons, charnel houses. Dazed children wandering the streets, searching for their parents. How can he explain to a girl, barely more than an infant, that the father and mother she sobs for are gone from this earth? Departed. Expired. They are resting, child. Asleep forever. In a far, far better place, my sweet, dear, suffering one. In God's bosom. Wrapped in His incorruptible arms. A dead mother with a dead baby at her breast. Piteous cries of the helpless offering all they own for a drink of water. How does he console the delirious boy who pummels him, fastens himself on his leg because he's put the boy's mother in a box and now must nail shut the lid?

Though light-headed from exhaustion, he's determined to spend a few hours here, among his own people. But were these lost ones really his people? The doors of his church were open to them, yet these were the ones who stayed away, wasting their lives in vicious pastimes of the idle, the unsaved, the ignorant. His benighted brethren who'd struggled to reach this city of refuge and then, once inside the gates, had fallen, prisoners again, trapped by chains of dissolute living as they'd formerly been snared in the bonds of slavery. He'd come here and preached to them. Thieves, beggars, loose women, debtors, fugitives, drunkards, gamblers, the weak, crippled and outcast with nowhere else to go. They spurned his church so he'd brought church to them, preaching in gin mills, whoring dens, on street corners. He'd been jeered and hooted, spat upon, clods of unnameable filth had spattered his coat. But a love for them, as deep and unfathomable as his sorrow, his pity, brought him back again and again, exhorting them, setting the gospel before them so they might partake of its bounty, the infinite goodness, blessed sustenance therein. Jesus had toiled among the wretched, the outcast, that flotsam and jetsam deposited like a ledge of filth on the banks of the city. He understood what had brought the dark faces of his brethren north, to the Quaker promise of this town, this cradle and capital of a New World, knew the misery they were fleeing, the bright star in the Gourd's handle that guided them, the joy leaping in their hearts when at last, at last the opportunity to be viewed as men instead of things was theirs. He'd dreamed such dreams himself, oh yes, and prayed that the light of hope would never be extinguished. He'd been praying for deliverance, for peace and understanding when God had granted him a vision, hordes of sable bondsmen throwing off their chains, marching, singing, a path opening in the sea, the sea shaking its shaggy shoulders, resplendent with light and power. A radiance sparkling in this walkway through the water, pearls, diamonds, spears of light. This was the glistening way home. Waters parting, glory blinking and winking. Too intense to stare at, a promise shimmering, a rainbow arching over the end of the path. A hand tapped him. He'd waited for it to blend into the vision, for its meaning to shine forth in the language neither word nor thought, God was speaking in His visitation. Tapping became a grip. Someone was shoving him. He was being pushed off his knees, hauled to his feet. Someone was snatching him from the honeyed dream of salvation. When his eyes popped open he knew the name of each church elder manhandling him. Pale faces above a wall of black cloth belonged to his fellow communicants. He knew without looking the names of the men whose hands touched him gently, steering, coaxing, and those whose hands dug into his flesh, the impatient, imperious, rough hands that shunned any contact with him except as overseer or master.

Allen, Allen. Do you hear me? You and your people must not kneel at the front of the gallery. On your feet. Come. Come. Now. On your feet.

Behind the last row of pews. There ye may fall down on your knees and give praise.

And so we built our African house of worship. But its walls could not imprison the Lord's word. Go forth. Go forth. And he did so. To this sinful quarter. Tunnels, cellars and caves. Where no sunlight penetrates. Where wind off the river cuts like a knife. Chill of icy spray channeled here from the ocean's wintry depths. Where each summer the brackish sea that is mouth and maw and bowel deposits its waste in puddles stinking to high heaven.

Water Street becomes what it's named, rises round his ankles, soaks his boots, threatens to drag him down. Patrolling these murky depths he's predator, scavenger, the prey of some dagger-toothed creature whose shadow closes over him like a net.

When the first settlers arrived here they'd scratched caves into the soft earth of the riverbank. Like ants. Rats. Gradually they'd pushed inland, laying out a geometrical grid of streets, perpendicular, true angled and straight edged, the mirror of their rectitude. Black Quaker coats and dour visages were remembrances of mud, darkness, the place of their lying in, cocooned like worms, propagating dreams of a holy city. The latest comers must always start here, on this dotted line, in this riot of alleys, lanes, tunnels. Wave after wave of immigrants unloaded here, winnowed here, dying in these shanties, grieving in strange languages. But white faces move on, bury their dead, bear their children, negotiate the invisible reef between this broken place and the foursquare town. Learn enough of their new tongue to say to the blacks they've left behind, *thou shalt not pass.*

I watched him bring the scalding liquid to his lips and thought to myself that's where his color comes from. The black brew he drinks every morning. Coloring him, changing him. A hue I had not considered until that instant as other than absence, something nonwhite and therefore its opposite, what light would be if extinguished, sky or sea drained of the color blue when the sun disappears, the blackness of cinders. As he sips, steam rises. I peer into the cup that's become mine, at the moon in its center, waxing, waning. A light burning in another part of the room caught there, as my face would be if I leaned over the cup's hot mouth. But I have no wish to see my face. His is what I study as I stare into my cup and see not absence, but the presence of wood darkly stained, wet plowed earth, a boulder rising from a lake, blackly glistening as it sheds crowns and beards and necklaces of water. His color neither neglect nor abstention, nor mystery, but a swelling tide in his skin of this bitter morning beverage it is my habit to imbibe.

We were losing, clearly losing the fight. One day in mid-September fifty-seven were buried before noon.

He'd begun with no preamble. Our conversation taken up again directly as if the months since our last meeting were no more than a cobweb his first words lightly brush away. I say conversation but a better word would be soliloquy because I was only a listener, a witness learning his story, a story buried so deeply he couldn't recall it, but dreamed pieces, a conversation with himself, a reverie with the power to sink us both into its unreality. So his first words did not begin the story where I remembered him ending it in our last session, but picked up midstream the ceaseless play of voices only he heard, always, summoning him, possessing him, enabling him to speak, to be.

Despair was in my heart. The fiction of our immunity had been exposed for the vicious lie it was, a not so subtle device for wresting us from our homes, our loved ones, the afflicted among us, and sending us to aid strangers. First they blamed us, called the sickness Barbados fever, a contagion from those blood-soaked islands, brought to these shores by refugees from the fighting in Santo Domingo. We were not welcome anywhere. A dark skin was seen not only as a badge of shame for its wearer. Now we were evil incarnate, the mask of long agony and violent death. Black servants were discharged. The draymen, carters, barbers, caterers, oyster sellers, street vendors could find no custom. It mattered not that some of us were born here and spoke no language but the English language, second-, even third-generation African Americans who knew no other country, who laughed at the antics of newly landed immigrants, Dutchmen, Welshmen, Scots, Irish, Frenchmen who had turned our marketplaces into Babel, stomping along in their clodhopper shoes, strange costumes, haughty airs, Lowlander gibberish that sounded like men coughing or dogs barking. My fellow countrymen searching every-

where but in their own hearts, the foulness upon which this city
is erected, to lay blame on others for the killing fever, pointed
their fingers at foreigners and called it Palatine fever, a pestilence imported from those low countries in Europe where, I
have been told, war for control of the sea-lanes, the human
cargoes transported thereupon, has raged for a hundred years.

But I am losing the thread, the ironical knot I wished to
untangle for you. How the knife was plunged in our hearts,
then cruelly twisted. We were proclaimed carriers of the fever
and treated as pariahs, but when it became expedient to com-
mand our services to nurse the sick and bury the dead, the
previous allegations were no longer mentioned. Urged on by
desperate counselors, the mayor granted us a blessed immunity. We were ordered to save the city.

I swear to you, and the bills of mortality, published by the
otherwise unreliable Mr. Carey, support my contention, that
the fever dealt with us severely. Among the city's poor and
destitute the fever's ravages were most deadly and we are always
the poorest of the poor. If an ordinance forbidding ringing
of bells to mourn the dead had not been passed, that awful
tolling would have marked our days, the watches of the night
in our African American community, as it did in those envi-
rons of the city we were forbidden to inhabit. Every morning
before I commenced my labors for the sick and dying, I would
hear moaning, screams of pain, fearful cries and supplications,
a chorus of lamentations scarring daybreak, my people awak-
ening to a nightmare that was devouring their will to live.

The small strength I was able to muster each morning
was sorely tried the moment my eyes and ears opened upon
the sufferings of my people, the reality that gave the lie to
the fiction of our immunity. When my duties among the whites
were concluded, how many nights did I return and struggle

till dawn with victims here, my friends, parishioners, wandering sons of Africa whose faces I could not look upon without seeing my own. I was commandeered to rise and go forth to the general task of saving the city, forced to leave this neighborhood where my skills were sorely needed. I nursed those who hated me, deserted the ones I loved, who loved me.

I recite the story many, many times to myself, let many voices speak to me till one begins to sound like the sea or rain or my feet those mornings shuffling through thick dust.

We arrived at Bush Hill early. To spare ourselves a long trek in the oppressive heat of day. Yellow haze hung over the city. Plumes of smoke from blazes in Potter's Field, from fires on street corners curled above the rooftops, lending the dismal aspect of a town sacked and burned. I've listened to the Santo Domingans tell of the burning of Cap François. How the capital city was engulfed by fires set in cane fields by the rebelling slaves. Horizon in flames all night as they huddled offshore in ships, terrified, wondering where next they'd go, if any port would permit them to land, empty-handed slaves, masters whose only wealth now was naked black bodies locked in the hold, wide-eyed witnesses of an empire's downfall, chanting, moaning, uncertain as the sea rocked them, whether or not anything on earth could survive the fearful conflagration consuming the great city of Cap François.

    Dawn breaking on a smoldering landscape, writhing columns of smoke, a general cloud of haze the color of a fever victim's eyes. I turn and stare at it a moment, then fall in

again with my brother's footsteps trudging through untended
fields girding Bush Hill.

From a prisoner-of-war ship in New York harbor where the
British had interned him he'd seen that city shed its graveclothes of fog. Morning after morning it would paint itself
damp and gray, a flat sketch on the canvas of sky, a tentative,
shivering screen of housefronts, sheds, sprawling warehouses
floating above the river. Then shadows and hollows darkened.
A jumble of masts, spars, sails began to sway, little boats plied
lanes between ships, tiny figures inched along wharves and
docks, doors opened, windows slid up or down, lending an
illusion of depth and animation to the portrait. This city in-
finitely beyond his reach, this charade other men staged to
mock him, to mark the distance he could not travel, the shore
he'd never reach, the city, so to speak, came to life and with
its birth each morning dropped the palpable weight of his
despair. His loneliness and exile. Moored in pewter water, on
an island that never stopped moving but never arrived anywhere. The city a mirage of light and air, chimera of paint,
brush and paper, mattered naught except that it was denied
him. It shimmered. Tolled. Unsettled the watery place where
he was sentenced to dwell. Conveyed to him each morning
the same doleful tidings: *The dead are legion, the living a
froth on dark, layered depths. But you are neither, and less
than both.* Each night he dreamed it burning, razed the city
till nothing remained but a dry, black crust, crackling, crunch-
ing under his boots as he strides, king of the nothing he surveys.

We passed holes dug into the earth where the sick are interred. Some died in these shallow pits, awash in their own vomited and voided filth, before a bed in the hospital could be made ready for them. Others believed they were being buried alive, and unable to crawl out, howled till reason or strength deserted them. A few, past caring, slept soundly in these ditches, resisted the attendants sent to rouse them and transport them inside, once they realized they were being resurrected to do battle again with the fever. I'd watched the red-bearded French doctor from Santo Domingo with his charts and assistants inspecting this zone, his *salle d'attente* he called it, greeting and reassuring new arrivals, interrogating them, nodding and bowing, hurrying from pit to pit, peering down at his invisible patients like a gardener tending seeds.

An introduction to the grave, a way into the hospital that prefigured the way most would leave it. That's what this bizarre rite of admission had seemed at first. But through this and other peculiar stratagems, Deveze, with his French practice, had transformed Bush Hill from lazarium to a clinic where victims of the fever, if not too weak upon arrival, stood a chance of surviving.

The cartman employed by Bush Hill had suddenly fallen sick. Faithful Wilcox had never missed a day, ferrying back and forth from town to hospital, hospital to Potter's Field. Bush Hill had its own cemetery now. Daily rations of dead could be disposed of less conspicuously in a plot on the grounds of the estate, screened from the horror-struck eyes of the city. No one had trusted the hospital. Tales of bloody chaos reigning there had filtered back to the city. Citizens believed it was a place where the doomed were stored until they died. Fever victims would have to be dragged from their beds into Bush Hill's cart. They'd struggle and scream, pitch themselves from the rolling cart, beg for help when the cart passed a rare pedestrian daring or foolish enough to be abroad in the deadly streets.

I wondered for the thousandth time why some were stricken, some not. Dr. Rush and this Deveze dipped their hands into the entrails of corpses, stirred the black, corrupted blood, breathed infected vapors exhaled from mortified remains. I'd observed both men steeped in noxious fluids expelled by their patients, yet neither had fallen prey to the fever. Stolid, dim Wilcox maintained daily concourse with the sick and buried the dead for two months before he was infected. They say a woman, undiscovered until boiling stench drove her neighbors into the street crying for aid, was the cause of Wilcox's downfall. A large woman, bloated into an even more cumbersome package by gases and liquids seething inside her body, had slipped from his grasp as he and another had hoisted her up into the cart. Catching against a rail, her body had slammed down and burst, spraying Wilcox like a fountain. Wilcox did not pride himself on being the tidiest of men, nor did his job demand one who was overfastidious, but the reeking stench from that accident was too much even for him and he departed in a huff to change his polluted garments. He never returned. So there I was at Bush Hill, where Rush had assigned me with my brother, to bury the flow of dead that did not ebb just because the Charon who was their familiar could no longer attend them.

The doctors believe they can find the secret of the fever in the victims' dead bodies. They cut, saw, extract, weigh, measure. The dead are carved into smaller and smaller bits and the butchered parts studied but they do not speak. What I know of the fever I've learned from the words of those I've treated, from stories of the living that are ignored by the good doctors. When lancet and fleam bleed the victims, they offer up stories like prayers.

It was a jaunty day. We served our white guests and after they'd eaten, they served us at the long, linen-draped tables. A sumptuous feast in the oak grove prepared by many and willing hands. All the world's eyes seemed to be watching us. The city's leading men, black and white, were in attendance to celebrate laying the cornerstone of St. Thomas Episcopal African Church. In spite of the heat and clouds of mettlesome insects, spirits were high. A gathering of whites and blacks in good Christian fellowship to commemorate the fruit of shared labor. Perhaps a new day was dawning. The picnic occurred in July. In less than a month the fever burst upon us.

When you open the dead, black or white, you find: the dura mater covering the brain is white and fibrous in appearance. The leptomeninges covering the brain are clear and without opacifications. The brain weighs 1450 grams and is formed symmetrically. Cut sections of the cerebral hemispheres reveal normal-appearing gray matter throughout. The white matter of the corpus callosum is intact and bears no lesions. The basal ganglia are in their normal locations and grossly appear to be without lesions. The ventricles are symmetrical and filled with crystal-clear cerebrospinal fluid.

The cerebellum is formed symmetrically. The nuclei of the cerebellum are unremarkable. Multiple sections through the pons, medulla oblongata and upper brain stem reveal normal gross anatomy. The cranial nerves are in their normal locations and unremarkable.

The muscles of the neck are in their normal locations. The cartilages of the larynx and the hyoid bone are intact. The thyroid and parathyroid glands are normal on their external surface. The mucosa of the larynx is shiny, smooth and without lesions. The vocal cords are unremarkable. A small amount of bloody material is present in the upper trachea.

The heart weighs 380 grams. The epicardial surface is smooth, glistening and without lesions. The myocardium of the left ventricle and septum are of a uniform meaty-red, firm appearance. The endocardial surfaces are smooth, glistening and without lesions. The auricular appendages are free from thrombi. The valve leaflets are thin and delicate, and show no evidence of vegetation.

The right lung weighs 400 grams. The left lung 510 grams. The pleural surfaces of the lungs are smooth and glistening.

The esophageal mucosa is glistening, white and folded. The stomach contains a large amount of black, noxious bile. A veriform appendix is present. The ascending, transverse and descending colon reveal hemorrhaging, striations, disturbance of normal mucosa patterns throughout. A small amount of bloody, liquid feces is present in the ano-rectal canal.

The liver weighs 1720 grams. The spleen weighs 150 grams. The right kidney weighs 190 grams. The left kidney weighs 180 grams. The testes show a glistening white tunica albuginea. Sections are unremarkable.

Dr. Rush and his assistants examined as many corpses as possible in spite of the hurry and tumult of never-ending attendance on the sick. Rush hoped to prove his remedy, his analysis of the cause and course of the fever correct. Attacked on all sides by his medical brethren for purging and bleeding patients already in a drastically weakened state, Rush lashed back at his detractors, wrote pamphlets, broadsides, brandished the stinking evidence of his postmortems to demonstrate conclusively how the sick drowned in their own poisoned fluids. The putrefaction, the black excess, he proclaimed, must be drained away, else the victim inevitably succumbs.

Dearest:

I shall not return home again until this business of the fever is terminated. I fear bringing the dread contagion into our home. My life is in the hands of God and as long as He sees fit to spare me I will persist in my labors on behalf of the sick, dying and dead. We are losing the battle. Eighty-eight were buried this past Thursday. I tremble for your safety. Wish the lie of immunity were true. Please let me know by way of a note sent to the residence of Dr. Rush that you and our dear Martha are well. I pray every hour that God will preserve you both. As difficult as it is to rise each morning and go with Thomas to perform our duties, the task would be unbearable if I did not hold in my heart a vision of these horrors ending, a blessed shining day when I return to you and drop this weary head upon your sweet bosom.

Allen, Allen, he called to me. Observe how even after death, the body rejects this bloody matter from nose and bowel and mouth. Verily, the patient who had expired at least an hour before, continued to stain the cloth I'd wrapped round him. We'd searched the rooms of a regal mansion, discovering six members of a family, patriarch, son, son's wife and three children, either dead or in the last frightful stages of the disease. Upon the advice of one of Dr. Rush's most outspoken critics, they had refused mercury purges and bleeding until now, when it was too late for any earthly remedy to preserve them. In the rich furnishings of this opulent mansion, attended by one remaining servant whom fear had not driven away, three generations had withered simultaneously, this proud family's link to past and future cut off absolutely, the great circle broken. In the first bedroom we'd entered we'd found William Spurgeon, merchant, son and father, present manager of the family fortune, so weak he could not speak, except with pained blinks of his terrible golden eyes. Did he welcome us? Was he apologizing to good Dr. Rush for doubting his cure? Did he fear the dark faces of my brother and myself? Quick, too quickly, he was gone. Answering no questions. Revealing nothing of his state of mind. A savaged face frozen above the blanket. Ancient beyond years. Jaundiced eyes not fooled by our busy ministrations, but staring through us, fixed on the eternal stillness soon to come. And I believe I learned in that yellow cast of his eyes, the exact hue of the sky, if sky it should be called, hanging over the next world where we abide.

Allen, Allen. He lasted only moments and then I wrapped him in a sheet from the chest at the foot of his canopied bed. We lifted him into a humbler litter, crudely nailed together, the lumber still green. Allen, look. Stench from the coffin cut through the oppressive odors permeating this doomed household. See. Like an infant the master of the house had soiled his swaddling clothes. Seepage formed a dark river and dripped between roughly jointed boards. We found his wife where she'd fallen, naked, yellow above the waist, black below.

As always the smell presaged what we'd discover behind a closed door. This woman had possessed closets of finery, slaves who dressed, fed, bathed and painted her, and yet here she lay, no one to cover her modesty, to lift her from the floor. Dr. Rush guessed from the discoloration she'd been dead two days, a guess confirmed by the loyal black maid, sick herself, who'd elected to stay when all others had deserted her masters. The demands of the living too much for her. She'd simply shut the door on her dead mistress. No breath, no heartbeat, Sir. I could not rouse her, Sir. I intended to return, Sir, but I was too weak to move her, too exhausted by my labors, Sir. Tears rolled down her creased black face and I wondered in my heart how this abused and despised old creature in her filthy apron and turban, this frail, worn woman, had survived the general calamity while the strong and pampered toppled round her.

I wanted to demand of her why she did not fly out the door now, finally freed of her burden, her lifelong enslavement to the whims of white people. Yet I asked her nothing. Considered instead myself, a man who'd worked years to purchase his wife's freedom, then his own, a so-called freeman, and here I was following in the train of Rush and his assistants, a functionary, a lackey, insulted daily by those I risked my life to heal.

Why did I not fly? Why was I not dancing in the streets, celebrating God's judgment on this wicked city? Fever made me freer than I'd ever been. Municipal government had collapsed. Anarchy ruled. As long as fever did not strike me I could come and go anywhere I pleased. Fortunes could be amassed in the streets. I could sell myself to the highest bidder, as nurse or undertaker, as surgeon trained by the famous Dr. Rush to apply his lifesaving cure. Anyone who would enter houses where fever was abroad could demand outrageous sums for negligible services. To be spared the fever was a chance for anyone, black or white, to be a king.

So why do you follow him like a loyal puppy, you confounded black fool? He wagged his finger. *You* ... His finger a gaunt, swollen-jointed, cracked-bone, chewed thing. Like the nose on his face. The nose I'd thought looked more like finger than nose. *Fool. Fool.* Finger wagging, then the cackle. The barn-yard braying. Berserk chickens cackling in his skinny, goiter-knobbed throat. You are a fool, you black son of Ham. You slack-witted, Nubian ape. You progeny of Peeping Toms and orangutans. Who forces you to accompany that madman Rush on his murderous tours? He kills a hundred for every one he helps with his lamebrain, nonsensical, unnatural, San-grado cures. Why do you tuck your monkey tail between your legs and skip after that butcher? Are you his shadow, a mindless, spineless black puddle of slime with no will of its own?

You are a good man, Allen. You worry about the souls of your people in this soulless wilderness. You love your family and your God. You are a beacon and steadfast. Your fatal flaw is narrowness of vision. You cannot see beyond these shores. The river, that stinking gutter into which the city shov-els its shit and extracts its drinking water, that long-suffering string of spittle winds to an ocean. A hundred miles down-stream the foamy mouth of the land sucks on the Atlantic's teat, trade winds saunter and a whole wide world awaits the voyager. I know, Allen. I've been everywhere. Buying and sell-ing everywhere.

If you would dare be Moses to your people and lead

them out of this land, you'd find fair fields for your talent.
Not lapdogging or doggy-trotting behind or fetch doggy or lie
doggy or doggy open your legs or doggy stay still while I beat
you. Follow the wound that is a river back to the sea. Be gone,
be gone. While there's still time. If there is time, *mon frère*.
If the pestilence has not settled in you already, breathed from
my foul guts into yours, even as we speak.

Here's a master for you. A real master, Allen. The fever that's
supping on my innards. I am more slave than you've ever
been. I do its bidding absolutely. Cough up my lungs. Shit
hunks of my bowel. When I die, they say my skin will turn as
black as yours, Allen.

     Return to your family. Do not leave them again. What-
ever the Rushes promise, whatever they threaten.

Once, ten thousand years ago I had a wife and children. I was
like you, Allen, proud, innocent, forward looking, well-spoken,
well-mannered, a beacon and steadfast. I began to believe the
whispered promise that I could have more. More of what, I
didn't ask. Didn't know, but I took my eyes off what I loved
in order to obtain this more. Left my wife and children and
when I returned they were gone. Forever lost to me. The
details are not significant. Suffice to say the circumstances of
my leaving were much like yours. Very much like yours, Allen.
And I lost everything. Became a wanderer among men. Bad
news people see coming from miles away. A pariah. A joke.
I'm not black like you, Allen. But I will be soon. Sooner than
you'll be white. And if you're ever white, you'll be as dead as
I'll be when I'm black.

Why do you desert your loved ones? What impels you to do what you find so painful, so unjust? Are you not a man? And free?

Her sleepy eyes, your lips on her warm cheek, each time may be the last meeting on this earth. The circumstances are similar, my brother. My shadow. My dirty face.

The dead are legion, the living a froth on dark, layered depths.

Master Abraham. There's a gentleman to see you, Sir. The golden-haired lad bound to me for seven years was carted across the seas, like you, Allen, in the bowels of a leaky tub. A son to replace my son his fathers had clubbed to death when they razed the ghetto of Antwerp. But I could not tame the inveterate hate, his aversion and contempt for me. From my aerie, at my desk secluded among barrels, bolts, crates and trunks of the shop's attic, I watched him steal, drink, fornicate. I overheard him denounce me to a delegate sent round to collect a tithe during the emergency. 'Tis well known in the old country that Jews bring the fever. Palatine fever that slays whole cities. They carry it under dirty fingernails, in the wimples of lizardy private parts. Pass it on with the evil eye. That's why we hound them from our towns, exterminate them. Beware of Master Abraham's glare. And the black-coated vulture listened intently. I could see him toting up the account in his small brain. Kill the Jew. Gain a shop and sturdy prentice, too. But I survived till fever laid me low and the cart brought me here to Bush Hill. For years he robbed and betrayed me and all my revenge was to treat him better. Allow him to pilfer, lie, embezzle. Let him grow fat and careless as I knew he would. With a father's boundless kindness I destroyed him. The last sorry laugh coming when I learned he died in agony, fever shriven, following by a day his Water Street French whore my indulgence allowed him to keep.

In Amsterdam I sold diamonds, Allen. In Barcelona they plucked hairs from my beard to fashion charms that brought ill fortune to their enemies. There were nights in dungeons when the mantle of my suffering was all I possessed to wrap round me and keep off mortal cold. I cursed God for choosing me, choosing my people to cuckold and slaughter. Have you heard of the Lamed-Vov, the Thirty Just Men set apart to suffer the reality humankind cannot bear? Saviors. But not Gods like your Christ. Not magicians, not sorcerers with bags of tricks, Allen. No divine immunities. Flesh and blood saviors. Men like we are, Allen. If man you are beneath your sable hide. Men who cough and scratch their sores and bleed and stink. Whose teeth rot. Whose wives and children are torn from them. Who wander the earth unable to die, but men always, men till God plucks them up and returns them to His side where they must thaw ten centuries to melt the crust of earthly grief and misery they've taken upon themselves. Ice men. Snowmen. I thought for many years I might be one of them. In my vanity. My self-pity. My foolishness. But no. One lifetime of sorrows enough for me. I'm just another customer. One more in the crowd lined up at his stall to purchase his wares.

You do know, don't you, Allen, that God is a bookseller? He publishes one book—the text of suffering—over and over again. He disguises it between new boards, in different shapes and sizes, prints on varying papers, in many fonts, adds prefaces and postscripts to deceive the buyer, but it's always the same book.

You say you do not return to your family because you don't want to infect them. Perhaps your fear is well-founded. But perhaps it also masks a greater fear. Can you imagine yourself, Allen, as other than you are? A free man with no charlatan Rush to blame. The weight of your life in your hands.

You've told me tales of citizens paralyzed by fear, of slaves on shipboard who turn to stone in their chains, their eyes boiled in the sun. Is it not possible that you suffer the converse of this immobility? You, sir, unable to stop an endless round of duty and obligation. Turning pages as if the next one or the next will let you finish the story and return to your life.

Your life, man. Tell me what sacred destiny, what nigger errand keeps you standing here at my filthy pallet? Fly, fly, fly away home. Your house is on fire, your children burning.

I have lived to see the slaves free. My people frolic in the streets. Black and white. The ones who believe they are either or both or neither. I am too old for dancing. Too old for foolishness. But this full moon makes me wish for two good legs. For three. Straddled a broomstick when I was a boy. Giddy-up, Giddy-up. Galloping m'lord, m'lady, around the yard I should be sweeping. Dust in my wake. Chickens squawking. My eyes everywhere at once so I would not be caught out by mistress or master in the sin of idleness. Of dreaming. Of following a child's inclination. My broom steed snatched away. Become a rod across my back. Ever cautious. Dreaming with one eye open. The eye I am now, old and gimpy limbed, watching while my people celebrate the rumor of Old Pharaoh's capitulation.

I've shed this city like a skin, wiggling out of it tenscore and more years, by miles and els, fretting, twisting. Many days I did not know whether I'd wrenched freer or crawled deeper into the sinuous pit. Somewhere a child stood, someplace green, keeping track, waiting for me. Hoping I'd meet him again, hoping my struggle was not in vain. I search that child's face for clues to my blurred features. Flesh drifted and banked, eroded by wind and water, the landscape of this city fitting me like a skin. Pray for me, child. For my unborn parents I carry in this orphan's potbelly. For this ancient face that slips like water through my fingers.

Night now. Bitter cold night. Fires in the hearths of lucky ones. Many of us still abide in dark cellars, caves dug into the earth below poor men's houses. For we are poorer still, burrow there, pull earth like blanket and quilt round us to shut out cold, sleep multitudes to a room, stacked and crosshatched and spoon fashion, ourselves the fuel, heat of one body passed to others and passed back from all to one. No wonder then the celebration does not end as a blazing chill sweeps off the Delaware. Those who leap and roar round the bonfires are better off where they are. They have no place else to go.

Given the derivation of the words, you could call the deadly, winged visitors an *unpleasantness from Egypt*.

Putrid stink rattles in his nostrils. He must stoop to enter the cellar. No answer as he shouts his name, his mission of mercy.

Earthen floor, ceiling and walls buttressed by occasional
beams, slabs of wood. Faint bobbing glow from his lantern.
He sees himself looming and shivering on the walls, a shadowy
presence with more substance than he feels he possesses at
this late hour. After a long day of visits, this hovel his last
stop before returning to his brother's house for a few hours
of rest. He has learned that exhaustion is a swamp he can
wade through and on the far side another region where a thin
trembling version of himself toils while he observes, bemused,
slipping in and out of sleep, amazed at the likeness, the skill
with which that other mounts and sustains him. Mimicry. Pup-
petry. Whatever controls this other, he allows the impostor to
continue, depends upon it to work when he no longer can.
After days in the city proper with Rush, he returns to these
twisting streets beside the river that are infected veins and
arteries he must bleed.

   At the rear of the cave, so deep in shadow he stumbles
against it before he sees it, is a mound of rags. When he leans
over it, speaking down into the darkness, he knows instantly
this is the source of the terrible smell, that something once
alive is rotting under the rags. He thinks of autumn leaves
blown into mountainous, crisp heaps, the north wind cleansing
itself and the city of summer. He thinks of anything, any
image that will rescue him momentarily from the nauseating
stench, postpone what he must do next. He screams no, no to
himself as he blinks away his wife's face, the face of his daughter. His neighbors had promised to check on them, he hears
news almost daily. There is no rhyme or reason in whom the
fever takes, whom it spares, but he's in the city every day,
exposed to its victims, breathing fetid air, touching corrupted
flesh. Surely if someone in his family must die, it will be him.
His clothes are drenched in vinegar, he sniffs the nostrum of

gunpowder, bark and asafetida in a bag pinned to his coat. He's prepared to purge and bleed himself, he's also ready and quite willing to forgo these precautions and cures if he thought surrendering his life might save theirs. He thinks and unthinks a picture of her hair, soft against his cheek, the wet warmth of his daughter's backside in the crook of his arm as he carries her to her mother's side where she'll be changed and fed. No. Like a choking mist, the smell of decaying flesh stifles him, forces him to turn away, once, twice, before he watches himself bend down into the brunt of it and uncover the sleepers.

Two Santo Domingan refugees, slave or free, no one knew for sure, inhabited this cellar. They had moved in less than a week before, the mother huge with child, man and woman both wracked by fever. No one knows how long the couple's been unattended. There was shame in the eyes and voices of the few from whom he'd gleaned bits and pieces of the Santo Domingans' history. Since no one really knew them and few nearby spoke their language, no one was willing to risk, et cetera. Except for screams one night, no one had seen or heard signs of life. If he'd been told nothing about them, his nose would have led him here.

He winces when he sees the dead man and woman, husband and wife, not entwined as in some ballad of love eternal, but turned back to back, distance between them, as if the horror were too visible, too great to bear, doubled in the other's eyes. What had they seen before they flung away from each other? If he could, he would rearrange them, spare the undertakers this vision.

Rat feet and rat squeak in the shadows. He'd stomped his feet, shooed them before he entered, hollered as he threw back the covers, but already they were accustomed to his presence, back at work. They'd bite indiscriminately, dead flesh, his flesh. He curses and flails his staff against the rags, strikes the earthen floor to keep the scavengers at bay. Those sounds are what precipitate the high-pitched cries that first frighten him, then shame him, then propel him to a tall packing crate turned on its end, atop which another crate is balanced. Inside the second wicker container, which had imported some item from some distant place into this land, twin brown babies hoot and wail.

We are passing over the Dismal Swamp. On the right is the Appalachian range, some of the oldest mountains on earth. Once there were steep ridges and valleys all through here but erosion off the mountains created landfill several miles deep in places. This accounts for the rich loamy soil of the region. Over the centuries several southern states were formed from this gradual erosion. The cash crops of cotton and tobacco so vital to southern prosperity were ideally suited to the fertile soil.

Yeah, I nurse these old funky motherfuckers, all right. White people, specially old white people, lemme tell you, boy, them peckerwoods stink. Stone dead fishy wet stink. Talking all the time bout niggers got BO. Well, white folks got the stink and gone, man. Don't be putting my hands on them, neither. Never. Huh uh. If I touch them, be wit gloves. They some nasty people, boy. And they don't be paying me enough to take no chances wit my health. Matter of fact they ain't paying me enough to really be expecting me to work. Yeah. Starvation wages. So I ain't hardly touching them. Or doing much else either. Got to smoke a cigarette to get close to some of them. Piss and shit theyselves like babies. They don't need much taking care anyway. Most of them three-quarters dead already. Ones that ain't is crazy. Nobody don't want them round, that's why they here. Talking to theyselves. Acting like they speaking to a roomful of people and not one soul in the ward paying attention. There's one old black dude, must be a hundred, he be muttering away to hisself nonstop everyday. Pitiful, man. Hope I don't never get that old. Shoot me, bro, if I start to getting old and fucked up in body and mind like them. Don't want no fools like me hanging over me when I can't do nothing no more for my ownself. Shit. They ain't paying me nothing so that's what I do. Nothing. Least I don't punch em or tease em or steal they shit like some the staff. And I don't pretend I'm God like these so-called professionals and doctors flittin round here drawing down that long bread. Naw. I just mind my own business, do my time. Cop a little TV, sneak me a joint when nobody's around. It ain't all that bad, really. Long as I ain't got no ole lady and crumb crushers. Don't know how the married cats make it on the little bit of chump change they pay us. But me, I'm free. It ain't that bad, really.

By the time his brother brought him the news of their deaths . . .

Almost an afterthought. The worst, he believed, had been overcome. Only a handful of deaths the last weeks of November. The city was recovering. Commerce thriving. Philadelphia must be revictualed, refueled, rebuilt, reconnected to the countryside, to markets foreign and domestic, to products, pleasures and appetites denied during the quarantine months of the fever. A new century would soon be dawning. We must forget the horrors. The Mayor proclaims a new day. Says let's put the past behind us. Of the eleven who died in the fire he said extreme measures were necessary as we cleansed ourselves of disruptive influences. The cost could have been much greater, he said I regret the loss of life, especially the half dozen kids, but I commend all city officials, all volunteers who helped return the city to the arc of glory that is its proper destiny.

When they cut him open, the one who decided to stay, to be a beacon and steadfast, they will find: liver (1720 grams), spleen (150 grams), right kidney (190 grams), left kidney (180 grams), brain (1450 grams), heart (380 grams) and right next to his heart, the miniature hand of a child, frozen in a grasping gesture, fingers like hard tongues of flame, still reaching for the marvel of the beating heart, fascinated still, though the heart is cold, beats not, the hand as curious about this infinite stillness as it was about thump and heat and quickness.

NOTES

"Valaida"—Valaida Snow (c. 1900–1956), whose life and legend inspired this story, was a jazz trumpeteer, singer and dancer of immense talent. A short article about her appears in *Stormy Weather: The Music and Lives of a Century of Jazzwomen* (1984), by Linda Dahl, Pantheon Books, New York.

"Presents"—I first heard about a boy being given a guitar and prophecy by his grandmother on a recording by "Preacher" Solomon Burke.

"Little Brother"—My wife and love of my life, to whom this story is dedicated, suggested that my Aunt Geraldine's strange dog needed a biographer.

"Fever"—Absalom Jones and Richard Allen's "Narrative" (1794); Gary B. Nash's *Forging Freedom* (1988), Harvard University Press; and especially J. H. Powell's *Bring Out Your Dead* (1949), University of Pennsylvania Press, were useful sources for this meditation on history.

FOR THE BEST IN PAPERBACKS, LOOK FOR THE

In every corner of the world, on every subject under the sun, Penguin represents quality and variety—the very best in publishing today.

For complete information about books available from Penguin—including Pelicans, Puffins, Peregrines, and Penguin Classics—and how to order them, write to us at the appropriate address below. Please note that for copyright reasons the selection of books varies from country to country.

In the United Kingdom: For a complete list of books available from Penguin in the U.K., please write to *Dept E.P., Penguin Books Ltd, Harmondsworth, Middlesex, UB7 0DA*.

In the United States: For a complete list of books available from Penguin in the U.S., please write to *Dept BA, Penguin, Box 120, Bergenfield, New Jersey 07621-0120*.

In Canada: For a complete list of books available from Penguin in Canada, please write to *Penguin Books Ltd, 2801 John Street, Markham, Ontario L3R 1B4*.

In Australia: For a complete list of books available from Penguin in Australia, please write to the *Marketing Department, Penguin Books Ltd, P.O. Box 257, Ringwood, Victoria 3134*.

In New Zealand: For a complete list of books available from Penguin in New Zealand, please write to the *Marketing Department, Penguin Books (NZ) Ltd, Private Bag, Takapuna, Auckland 9*.

In India: For a complete list of books available from Penguin, please write to *Penguin Overseas Ltd, 706 Eros Apartments, 56 Nehru Place, New Delhi, 110019*.

In Holland: For a complete list of books available from Penguin in Holland, please write to *Penguin Books Nederland B.V., Postbus 195, NL-1380AD Weesp, Netherlands*.

In Germany: For a complete list of books available from Penguin, please write to *Penguin Books Ltd, Friedrichstrasse 10-12, D-6000 Frankfurt Main I, Federal Republic of Germany*.

In Spain: For a complete list of books available from Penguin in Spain, please write to *Longman, Penguin España, Calle San Nicolas 15, E-28013 Madrid, Spain*.

In Japan: For a complete list of books available from Penguin in Japan, please write to *Longman Penguin Japan Co Ltd, Yamaguchi Building, 2-12-9 Kanda Jimbocho, Chiyoda-Ku, Tokyo 101, Japan*.

☐ **THE WOMEN OF BREWSTER PLACE**
A Novel in Seven Stories
Gloria Naylor

Winner of the American Book Award, this is the story of seven survivors of an
urban housing project — a blind alley feeding into a dead end. From a variety of
backgrounds, they experience, fight against, and sometimes transcend the fate of
black women in America today.
                    192 pages   *ISBN: 0-14-006690-X*   **$5.95**

☐ **STONES FOR IBARRA**
Harriet Doerr

An American couple comes to the small Mexican village of Ibarra to reopen
a copper mine, learning much about life and death from the deeply faithful
villagers.   *214 pages*   *ISBN: 0-14-007562-3*   **$5.95**

☐ **WORLD'S END**
T. Coraghessan Boyle

"Boyle has emerged as one of the most inventive and verbally exuberant writers
of his generation," writes *The New York Times*. Here he tells the story of Walter
Van Brunt, who collides with early American history while searching for his lost
father.   *456 pages*   *ISBN: 0-14-009760-0*   **$8.95**

☐ **THE WHISPER OF THE RIVER**
Ferrol Sams

The story of Porter Osborn, Jr., who, in 1938, leaves his rural Georgia home to
face the world at Willingham University, *The Whisper of the River* is peppered
with memorable characters and resonates with the details of place and time. Ferrol Sams's writing is regional fiction at its best.
                    528 pages   *ISBN: 0-14-008387-1*   **$6.95**

☐ **ENGLISH CREEK**
Ivan Doig

Drawing on the same heritage he celebrated in *This House of Sky,* Ivan Doig creates a rich and varied tapestry of northern Montana and of our country in the late
1930s.   *338 pages*   *ISBN: 0-14-008442-8*   **$6.95**

☐ **THE YEAR OF SILENCE**
Madison Smartt Bell

A penetrating look at the varied reactions to a young woman's suicide exactly one
year later, *The Year of Silence* "captures vividly and poignantly the chancy dance
of life." (*The New York Times Book Review*)
                    208 pages   *ISBN: 0-14-011533-1*   **$6.95**